A Postcard FROM Jerusalem

A NOVEL

CORY J. SCHULMAN

A Postcard from Jerusalem

Cory J. Schulman

Germantown, Maryland

Best Seller Publications, LLC
Copyright © 2024 Cory J. Schulman

Cover Design: Lori Schulman

Library of Congress Cataloging-in-Publication Data

Names: Cory J. Schulman, 1963-Present.
Title: *A Postcard from Jerusalem*
Description: Trade paperback edition.
Maryland : Best Seller Publications, LLC, 2024.
Identifiers: LCCN 2024902781
            ISBN 978-0-9642997-4-0 (softcover)

Subjects: A group of American teenagers travel to Israel for a six-month adventure and self-discovery.

BISAC: FIC000000   FICTION / General

Printed in the United States of America

BestSellerPublications.com

BestSellerPublications@gmail.com

Also by Cory J. Schulman:

The Writer's Story

When Time Was Endless

The World of Comics

Textbook Follies

Other books published by BSP:

Dual Mission

Living With Madness

Ex-Cops and Robbers

Messages to the author or publisher may be sent to BestSellerPublications@gmail.com

Dedication

To those who work toward peace in

the Middle East

Quotation

"Any man who can drive safely while kissing a pretty girl is simply not giving the kiss the attention it deserves."

—Albert Einstein

Table of Contents

5

Chapter 1: The Group and the Journey

Ahava captivated my imagination at first sight. She stood in a circle with other members of our travel group. We were all complete strangers. Yet, she meshed seamlessly with a tall, handsome young buck who I would come to know as Ezra, my soon to be good friend and archnemesis. She smiled delightfully in his company and attention, while cutely nibbling her fingernail in a subconscious anxiety.

Ahava's teeth were perfectly aligned, which she revealed in an occasional smile that complemented her sparkling eyes. Her face beamed in connection with another, relinquishing all need for makeup. She was a natural beauty with long brown hair that she tied with a bandanna.

Despite my interest to enter the social domain, I watched her from a distance like a wallflower, as the others mingled. I watched them as if I were at a zoo standing before an exhibit of monkeys, fascinated by the simplest of primate interactions and behaviors such as nervous biting of one's nails or combing fingers through one's hair. I heard sharp bursts of laughter, which piqued my curiosity: I couldn't hear what was said, but I couldn't imagine what anybody could say at the first moments of meeting another that could produce such laughter. After a few panicky seconds, I concluded that the young man had a gift for gab and knew how to make a welcoming first impression, even with an unjustifiable laugh, which was probably all nervous gesture and nothing really warranted.

Frustrated with my own inhibitions, I broke my intense focus from Ahava and Ezra to glance about and take in my environment. We were about 15 coeds ages 16 through 18 years old, collected from all over the United States to participate in a 6-month sojourn and adventure in Israel. We all met for the first time, here at LaGuardia Airport in New York. As with any random group of 15, smaller groups formed, which were the genesis of future cliques, close friendships, lovers, and in my case—a love triangle.

Seeing Ahava and Ezra in the flirtatious state rankled me, even though I had no claim to her, nor any invested experience—not even an initial introduction. Yet, in my heart, I knew I must have her. And like an experienced wild-game hunter, my mind calculated that it wasn't my time and that I would have to advance with great caution and patience to win her. When Ahava removed her heavy down-filled coat, her shape revealed a full-breasted chest, a flat stomach and well-defined waist, which narrowed from rolling hips. For a young woman of age, she burst with mature ripeness and innocence at the same time.

Ahava wasn't the only one who commanded attention without effort. Other young women cackled in their own circles with other young men whose bodies could almost all be interchanged with one another: lean and brawny with a whole head of hair mopped in curls or swept to the side. At the peak of our sexual and physical identities, our male forms were more or less similar with exception of the outliers: Gabriel, whose height and brawn was anchored with a chiseled face that belonged on a Hollywood movie poster; and Brent, who was the only pudgy male amongst us.

On the female ledger, there was Leah, who was, politely speaking, vastly overweight, and Diana, who was a force of nature with her audacious physique and words that came out of her mouth as if she used a bullhorn. She was *zoftig*, a large, curvaceous, busty woman who wouldn't be caught dead without eyeliner, sharp red lipstick, and high heels, to mention just a few idiosyncrasies. Diana had to be angrily convinced not to wear high heels to the desert hike. To clarify, Diana got what she wanted, always. Her only fault was that she was unlikable. There was also Abigail, the only curly blonde, and Hannah, both vivacious, petite, and attractive.

At this juncture, we were all eligible bachelors and bachelorettes in a pool of people who were yet to differentiate themselves from each other no differently than one quart of liquid from another quart of liquid. It would take time to see who fermented into Chardonnay, and who would just evaporate and dissipate out of our consciousness. We were all Jewish, but it would take time and experiences to reveal our differences.

With my survey of the crowd continuing, I began to read the faces of our members. There was Daniel, who wore mirrored sunglasses indoors with a military-like crew cut. I overheard him talking about wanting to join the Israeli Army as his ultimate mission after the 6-month trip was over. He wanted to make "Aliyah," or join Israeli society as a citizen of the country. He soaked up the prestige of the famed Israeli muscle with nothing more than by uttering a desire for such an association, without any actual evidence of his commitment. But who's to tell the future? Now, with a simple proclamation of aspiration, but without any sacrifice or effort, he elevated his status to a soldier.

There was Steve, a hunky ladies' man with the coolness of a jazz musician. He always spoke slowly as if sloshed. And Aaron talked about sporting events. "I can't believe we're going to miss the Super Bowl," he whined, as if sitting on a couch eating barbecued wings watching the event would be life defining.

In another threesome, an obviously charismatic young man, David, charmed two young females with his magnetic smile and warm conversation about peace and vegetarianism. Despite only being 16, he carried himself with an old soul's confidence. His long, black hair draped down his spine was his silent way of expressing rebellion against the establishment. His embrace to speak out on societal ills captivated others as if he were a cult leader.

Abigail and Hannah listened attentively as David denounced the corruption and terroristic nature of the Palestinian leadership, Hamas, the PLO, and Hezbollah. Abigail was also an attractive 17-year-old who prided herself on scoring very high on the SATs. She said that after the trip was over, she would be enrolling in Tufts University, a highly competitive institution. Hannah, not wanting to be left out, chimed in that she spoke five languages and was looking forward to learning Hebrew with her natural ability to learn languages.

One odd-looking fellow, Gregory, skinny and bony, wore out-of-style plastic frames and thick lenses. He came across awkwardly as if autistic. I could only imagine what these peers thought of me, just idle and isolated. I wasn't integrating any more than the autistic kid. But a few of us were shy and not engaged in loud chatter.

Couplet and triplet groups chatted about the latest rising musician to strike a chord; their recent graduation from high school; which part of the US we each came from; and other innocuous topics.

Ahava was accompanied by her guitar, which would never leave her side, as if it were her conjoined twin. She opened up her guitar case and hung the strap around her neck, and strummed a delicate melody.

Brent lumbered over to her and said, "Hey, I brought my six-string too. Maybe we can jam together?" Again, an instant relationship of sorts sprouted from a common interest. They talked about guitar riffs and their song repertoire. Since Ahava had short fingernails because she often bit them, she didn't need to use a pick

From my protective stance, I assessed my peers as anonymously as if I were behind a one-way mirror. I homed in on their conversations, making associations: Ezra was a brainy one with a sense of humor. He was down to earth and held a paperback, *All the President's Men,* in his hand. I finally found someone who I believed was approachable for someone as shy as me, anyway. I approached Ezra, who also wore a curly mop of hair and glasses, and despite spying his book title already, I broke my silence by asking him, "Hey, what are you reading?" He held up the book so I could determine that for myself. I half-smiled and responded, "I saw the movie."

He replied, "The book is better." He hesitated as if acknowledging his response may have come across as inadvertently derisive. Then he added, "But Hoffman and Redford played their parts credibly." Then the conversation birthed a life of its own. Ezra asked, "Do you follow politics?"

I nervously wiped my nose and explained, "I just took Political Science 101. I'm Isaac, by the way."

"Ezra," he said to identify himself then blurted out, "You're in college already?"

"Yeah, I graduated high school a year early by taking English in the summer. That way I won't lose any time while I'm in Israel for the next 6 months."

"Which college are you going to?"

"Just a local community college. But it enables a convenient transition to a 4-year school." Anticipating the follow-up question, I continued, "I haven't decided on which one yet."

Ezra proudly volunteered, "I've been accepted to Brandeis University."

"How did you decide that?"

"The student population is about 35 percent Jewish, so…" He hesitated a moment to state what should be obvious. "I'll feel at home there. And it's a top school, pretty competitive."

"I don't know where I'm going to transfer to yet, probably the University of Maryland…just because it's close to my family's home and it's a decent school, also with a large Jewish population."

Abigail and Hannah instantly bonded over their love for stage musicals and broke out in song. One sung on pitch, but the other one was painfully offkey. They were also attractive, but for some indescribable reason, I wasn't smitten with either of them. I only had an affinity for Ahava. But their duet was a buoyant backdrop to our budding friendships on this overseas trip that was taking us away from the familiarities of country, family, and academics. We were embarking on an adventure of autonomy in another country, out of our familial cocoons, and on the verge of discovering ourselves without the social conscience imposed by our parents.

The discorded talk amongst ourselves blended in the atmosphere and became a harmonious chatter. At this point, the excitement of the group's interaction was penetrated by our group's travel guide who raised her hand and bellowed, "May I have your attention, please? I am Sharona. I will be your guide for the Adventure in Kibbutz trip to Israel for your duration in the country. I am American born, but was raised in Israel, and speak both English and Hebrew fluently. We will get to know each other over the coming weeks while we settle into our itinerary and travel throughout the cities, countryside, desert, and see the sights from our ancestral history. After we arrive in Israel, we will travel for 3 weeks by bus to see the sights. Then, as you know, we will each be 'adopted' by an assigned Israeli family to live in their homes. So, we will each live in a different home across Jerusalem for 3 months, where you will also learn Hebrew in an Ulpan, or language school. For the remainder of the trip, we will regroup to live and work on a kibbutz."

As my eyes panned the genesis of excited groupings, I heard laughter and hooting as we giddily awaited further direction to embark on our 11-hour ride on a 747 across the Atlantic to the land of Israel.

Chapter 2: El Al

Sharona, a matronly but still attractive woman in her late thirties, raised her voice so everyone could hear her over the ambient airport noise. "We must get our documents together to board the plane. To cross the Atlantic and arrive in Israel will take about 11 hours." The group groaned. Sharon continued, "We will fly on El Al's 747-400 over 5,760 miles and will land at Ben Gurion International Airport near Tel Aviv." She then led quick introductions of everyone and led the ragtag line of Americans each walking in tow with suitcases and winter coats and handbags and cameras hanging around their necks, looking very much like tourists. They went through security, supplying boarding tickets and passports to the attendants before embarking the jumbo airliner.

The group members were seated sporadically throughout the jet liner's cabin, which hosted nine seats across with as many rows to carry more than 500 passengers. Some of the passengers were Hasidic (pious) Jews whose ultra-orthodox attire presented an unmistakable appearance. They wore black garb with black fedora-like hats or a grander black hat called a Streimel, to cover their heads, especially when praying as a reminder that God is always above them. Hasidic men wore long, black beards and mustaches complemented with payos, long curly locks of hair draped down past their ears to comply with biblical teachings "that a man should not round the corner of his head," which has been interpreted over the ages as a haircutting restriction that must be obeyed.

Once the El Al plane took flight and soared to cloud level, a relaxed sigh of relief intermingled with anxiety of the unknown future. The sheer boredom sitting in coach during the 11-hour flight challenged us to mingle with others from the group despite preconceived notions about who we were. But even the most introverted passengers, at times, got approached by a livelier person. That's when Ahava unbuckled her seatbelt and walked along the corridor chatting with whoever responded to her. My eyes fixated on her and moved in synchrony with her walk down the aisle. I couldn't keep my eyes off of her and couldn't prevent my jealousies from rising upon witnessing her interaction with other group members.

Getting stiff in the neck from hours seated, I finally stood and climbed over the adjacent passenger to get to the aisle. I walked to the back of the plane to the bathroom, where I waited behind several others for access. When I came out, I took the opportunity to stretch to the floor, which evoked a minor achy groan. "Not keeping up with your yoga practice, huh?" Ahava teased as she approached me.

Not recognizing the sarcasm, I replied factually, "Oh, I don't do yoga."

"Yeah," she said and giggled infectiously. Her smile warmed my soul, and I maintained a nebbish stare into her dark brown eyes, knowing I was captivated.

"I heard you strum a bit on your guitar at the airport. I love the guitar sound." And for the first time since the trip began, I cracked a smile.

"Oh yeah, I bring my guitar everywhere I go. Do you play an instrument too?"

I scoffed in recognition of my many limitations for such talents, but managed to salvage face with deprecating humor. "Just the radio."

She cackled a bit, and a simple connection was born. "Well, what do you do well?" she probed.

"I play a lot of basketball?"

"I thought you had to be tall to play that."

I paused to reflect on that and in my nervousness, I uttered, "Well, I play in stilettos. That gives me three more inches. But they're not good for the parquet."

Recognizing my oblique, dead-pan humor this time, she lightly punched me in the arm, which constituted our first inkling of physical intimacy. "Do you always make jokes?"

"It's a nervous-reaction thing of mine."

"What do you have to be nervous about? Do I make you nervous, Isaac?"

"You know, Ahava, I just don't know anybody here yet. Not like David and Brent, who went to the same high school together," I said, citing the one factual thing I overheard about some group members.

"Most of us are from areas scattered across the US. Gabriel is from New Jersey like me."

"Neighbors, huh?"

"Not exactly, but I do know he's into karate," she mentioned.

"Oh," I replied at the mention of Gabriel, a driveling end to the conversation's momentum, and she began to look about the cabin to escape my presence, I gathered.

"Well, it was nice to talk one-on-one finally. I've nearly spoken to everyone, just need to see what Diana and Leah are about. I'll see you later, Isaac." And with that, she turned away as if she were a simple breeze that grazed my cheek and was suddenly gone.

My mind quickly tried to analyze the entire encounter. Did she really want to talk to me, or was she just making the rounds to get to know everyone? With that, she must have been speaking to me almost as an obligation. I concluded, I was simply an equal opportunity encounter that each of us in the group could expect from an extrovert like Ahava. Despite my doubts, I was still titillated by her soft pat on my arm. Maybe I just had to play it cool. I'll have 6 months' worth of opportunity, but then again so will all the other guys. I couldn't just wait my turn passively, or else one of these dudes was going to get her attention, like Gabriel or Ezra.

The flight was not even half way, when I realized I had snoozed, read, watched two movies, and was completely feeling captive in my seat. So, like many others, I climbed over the adjacent passenger and roamed the cabin, meandering about looking at people sleeping, watching their movie screens, quietly chatting. Near the back of the plane, Ezra stood in line to the bathroom. "Hey," I said, feeling more comfortable with him since we exchanged a few words at the airport.

Ezra returned a gracious smile and remembering our last conversation, continued it. "I finished *All the President's Men.*"

"Wow, that was fast. You are Brandeis material," I stroked. He laughed, then admitted that he is a voracious reader. We continued exchanging information about our lives from high school and our futures in college. But eventually the conversation came back to politics. He spoke excitedly about Israeli politics, but I couldn't keep up with him. Ezra was beyond his years and easily recounted what he knew about the Knesset (parliament), the Likud and Labor parties, and how the Israeli government is made of coalitions, since no one party was able to dominate the votes. I could offer nothing more, so I just nodded while taking in his lecture.

The hours passed with little more gained on the social front. The pilot's voice came over the speaker telling us we should return to our seats and buckle up to get ready to land at Ben Gurion Airport. The message was repeated in Hebrew and French. I felt immersed in the international scene for the first time. The plane deployed its air landing gear and descended. Suddenly the cabin full of passengers broke out in Jewish song: "Ha Va, Nagila Hava…" (Let us rejoice and be happy) and upon landing smoothly and stopping, the pilot said, "Welcome home."

Chapter 3: The Adventure

After we disembarked from the aircraft, we reassembled as a group with our guide, Sharona, who accounted for us all. She led us to a bus that brought us to a hotel where we settled for the night. Feeling the accumulation of 20 hours of sweat on our bodies, we took turns showering. Sharona told us not to use too much water…that we should turn off the shower faucet while soaping up to conserve water, given how precious a resource it is in Israel.

We were offered cold cheese between two slices of bread to hold our appetites until morning. "Are you kidding me? This is all we get to eat?" Gabriel and Brent openly complained at the sight of the sandwiches, believing for the price of the trip, we deserved a heartier meal. This was the first of many indicators that we were no longer in the "rich" United States, and that we would have to moderate our behaviors and expectations.

At 3:30 in the morning, we were awoken. The group assembled, still acclimating to jet lag. We groggily ate hard boiled eggs, then boarded the bus. We tried to nap on the bus ride to the desert, but it only gained us about 90 minutes of rest. The country is small and most trips didn't take too long to get to the desired destination.

We arrived at the base of Masada and the skies were still dark but peppered with billions of stars that one couldn't see from a city. Knowing little about this site, we obliged our leader and started hiking in a ragged line along a rocky path that ascended to the mountaintop. As we climbed farther up the mountainside in our most rugged boots, the skies began to promise light. Sharona timed our ascent perfectly as we huffed and puffed for about 20 minutes until reaching the 18-acre plateau at the top before the sun became visible. At the summit, we were met with mud and stone walls and rooms of an ancient refuge for Jewish citizens that were under siege by the powerful Roman army of its time.

We all stood at the remnant walls that remained waist high, and looked to the horizon. Moment after moment the sky lightened until the edge of the orange sun breached the horizon. A moment later the sunrays brightened until we could no longer witness its emergence with the naked eye. The sun shone and cast long shadows across the top of Masada.

Sharona called us to gather together so she could address us with the history that made this mountain a part of Jewish resistance against a powerful and merciless enemy. "We are standing on the top of Masada, which means 'strong foundation or support.' We are in the Judean desert about 400 meters higher than sea level," she began with a geographical orientation. "As you can see below and all around the mountain, it is desolate. Masada was once a fortress that supported a Jewish society with plenty of water and food. But how can this be when we are in a desert where no water or anything can live…where it is so barren?

"First the history of Masada. 'Herod the Great' was the King of Judea from the years 37 to 4 BC. The ruins you see before you were once a palace built by him. But when the Roman empire invaded Judea, this compound became a fortress against the strong Roman army. By being on top of a formidable mountain with a steep shear, it served the Masada Jews well against their enemies. The fortress was complete with storerooms, cisterns, and defensive walls that encircled the castle.

"After the Romans conquered Jerusalem in 70 AD, they sent troops to destroy the last Jewish holdout at Masada. Only 960 Jewish rebels, including women and children, resisted capture from 8,000 Roman troops who surrounded the mountain base.

"The Jews repelled attacks from the powerful Roman army for several months, until the Romans built a ramp made out of earth and wooden scaffolding, which enabled them to successfully penetrate the fortress walls. When the Roman invasion became imminent on April 15, 73 AD, all but a few Jews atop Masada committed suicide rather than become Roman slaves.

"Now that you know the history of Jewish resistance at Masada, feel free to roam the ruins: there are 29 rooms that once stored food and weapons. The inhabitants lived off of livestock, and rainwater that flowed into cisterns, which held more than 40,000 cubic meters of water, which could sustain the Masada population for years. King Herod had built a tall palace on the northern edge that overlooked the desert valley and Dead Sea. Herod also built bathhouses, a swimming pool, and a synagogue.

"There are also some artifacts from when Masada was occupied by the Byzantines in the fifth century. You will see the walls and floors of a Byzantine church decorated with colorful mosaics.

"The mountain was unoccupied for 13 centuries until it was rediscovered in 1828. Since then, archaeologists have uncovered many structures, a sophisticated water channeling system, and artifacts including papyrus scrolls."

Ahava's eyes met mine, which must have triggered a slight smile of mirth on my face because her face lit up again. It seemed to me that Ahava was the type of person who needed only the simplest of reasons to rejoice in giddiness. Then I thought, is she like this because of me or is she always reacting to people in a flirtatious manner? Maybe she was simply elated by the excitement of the trip and being in the moment at the site.

We met face to face, where I stood mesmerized by her hippy long hair and filled-out jeans and of course her inviting smile. Naturally, she lightly rapped my shoulder with her fist in a sign of familiarity and connection. "What d'you think about all this?" she asked.

I didn't have any stellar insights into the ruins other than what we all listened to from the tour guide, so I just commented positively, "It's quite remarkable that the Masada Jews lasted for so many months against the most powerful army in the world at that time."

"Do you know a lot about all this, Isaac?" she asked, hoping I was more scholarly than I actually was.

But I did have something relevant to say. "I just finished a course in ancient history at my college, but the textbook and professor never mentioned Masada, so I guess on the larger scale of world events, it wasn't such a seismic happening. But for Judaic history, I can see it as another example of both Jewish oppression and resistance."

"You're in college already?" Ahava asked with a sense of awe.

That's what she took from all that I could say about Masada? I was quite proud that I mustered anything to say. After a hesitation of disbelief, I managed to address her question. "Uh, yeah, I graduated a year early so I could go on this trip, but since it didn't start till February, I enrolled in my local college for the fall semester."

Believing we were missing out on the experience at Masada and that our chitchat could wait for another time, I suggested, "Would you like to roam around the ruins with me, Ahava?" Not replying verbally, she grabbed my arm, looping hers around mine as we meandered about the crowd of tourists at the mountaintop checking out the half-destroyed chambers and reconstructed walls of the complex.

I took snapshots of various structures and some of the group members. They posed as I got my first pictures of people I barely knew, but who held promise for becoming important in my life.

Ahava must have had the ability to immediately understand shy people because she initiated contact. If I were to do the same action, it would be considered a rude overstep of physical encroachment. At least that's what my inhibitions told me. So, I enjoyed her letting me off the hook by taking responsibility of that department. Any physical contact, I took as a win—regardless of whether Ahava was like this with everyone or just me.

I asked Ezra to take a picture of Ahava and me sitting on a half wall. Who knew, maybe we would become soul mates and last longer than did the resistance at Masada. We huddled as a threesome and exchanged words that strengthened our familiarity with one another. We talked about our families back home, siblings, and high schools. We talked about why we were interested in coming to Israel. And how religious we were raised. Ezra exuded the most knowledge of Judaism, asking, "Looks like nobody in the group is Orthodox, but what about you two? Are you Conservative, Reform, or secular agnostic/atheist?"

I replied first. "Well, I was raised by going to a Conservative synagogue, but my home was nonreligious, and I don't take to organized religion well. I even quit Hebrew school when I was 12 and didn't have a bar mitzvah."

Without judgment, but compelled to address the oddity, Ezra asked, "Why'd you quit?"

"All we did was read and try to memorize prayers in Hebrew. I never remembered the English translations, so it was all ritual without any meaning to me. All the students and I learned how to read Hebrew, but never learned to speak it as a language."

"So you thought you were just going through the motions, without feeling anything?" Ahava interjected.

"Right, exactly. Not only that but I had to go after public school twice a week, and on Saturdays. Homework for both public and Hebrew school was too taxing on me, personally anyway."

"So you didn't go through with a bar mitzvah?" Ezra asked nonjudgmentally.

"No, but that was mainly because of stage fright. I couldn't imagine trying to sing passages of the Torah in front of hundreds of family, friends, and other attendees," I admitted frankly.

"But you missed out on the cash gifts afterwards," he said.

"That's how petrified I was. You know what they say, public speaking is the number one fear, even over dying. So I'd rather be the one decomposing in the casket than the one composing the eulogy. What about you both? Did you go through with the ceremonies?"

Ezra spoke up first. "Yeah, we had a big party in DC."

"Why in DC? I thought you were from Boston?"

"My father invited a lot of his contacts from federal agencies from there. It was held at the famous Watergate hotel."

"Watergate!" I yelped at the mention of such a notorious reference.

"Yeah, I was actually expecting to see G. Gordon Liddy in the hallways. But hey, I was only 13."

"So what kind of gifts did you get: shredded documents?" Ahava and Ezra laughed.

"No, you know the usual: bonds, cash, checks. I had a few friends. Someone handed me a glass of water, but it was really vodka. I took a swallow then choked it out. They all thought that was hilarious."

"A little hazing, huh?"

Ezra then explained, "I felt more like a man when I went through my growth spurt. It seemed like every day when I woke up, I was taller and clumsier with each lumbering step of my giant feet." We all giggled at the expressive image.

Ahava volunteered, "I never had a bat mitzvah. My grandparents migrated from the Netherlands and wanted to assimilate into American culture, so my parents continued what my grandparents started, which was to copy the Christians. So, we had a Christmas tree every year and we exchanged gifts. It's only now that I'm here in Israel that I'm connecting with being Jewish."

"Christmas trees," I echoed in disbelief.

Ezra chimed in, "Yeah, a lot of immigrants do that, you know, to fit into the new culture."

Ahava continued, "And Christmas parties every year. My father owned several bookstores. So he used to invite a lot of potential business colleagues to our house and have a bash. It wasn't like we were engaged religiously. It was just a means to become integrated and connected with others. And since most of our social network were Christian, that's how we bent. Get it?"

"I get it. Being Jewish is different for everyone. It all depends on your influences," I said in support.

"And what do you want in the future?" she added.

"What do you mean?"

"Like how you want to raise children."

"Oh. Yeah, well, that's far off in my future. I guess I would have to get a girlfriend first."

Ahava blushed. Then she said, "There's someone for everyone."

"That's not something you have worry about," Ezra said to Ahava.

Ahava replied, "A lot of boys approach me, but usually they're the wrong type. They just want to get into my pants."

"Your pants wouldn't even fit me. I'm a good two inches taller than you," I quipped.

Ahava lightly punched me in the arm.

Sharona raised her hand and shouted over the compound, "Hey, everyone, we are about out of time. So let's return to the bus along this path," as she led the way.

Brent, who got to the bus first with Abigail, Hannah, and Aaron, took out his guitar and asked for requests. When most of us were huddled by the bus, someone yelled out "Dylan," so he played a Bob Dylan song that calmed the chatter among everyone still excited by the exposure to the two-thousand-year-old ruin. Abigail and Hannah ogled Gabriel, who stripped away his shirt under the claim of heat exhaustion, but really to expose the young ladies to his Adonis-like physique. He was naturally ripped, and he knew it, and in shape from karate practice. He opened a bottle of Coke and leaned back to hold the bottle vertically to his mouth as he chugged the contents until the bottle was empty. Afterward, he exerted an "Ahhhh," to exude how refreshing the beverage was, then burped. The young ladies in his company giggled.

Gregory, the autistic teen, straggled last in our group to reach the bus as the driver patiently waited while listening to the news. As Gregory stepped onto the bus, he overheard the radio announcer. He then shouted out, "Did you hear that!"

Several of us were alarmed by Gregory's outburst. "What happened?" someone asked.

"On the radio. A bus just blew up in Jerusalem."

Brent stopped strumming his guitar, and we all went silent to listen to the news report from the bus radio.

"Was anyone hurt?" another asked.

"I don't know. I just heard it on the radio. Just now, on the radio."

"We get it, Gregory. You heard it on the radio," Aaron said, irritated at Gregory's repetitive speech pattern and panicky disposition.

"Be kind to him; he's different," Hannah reprimanded to openly show support for Gregory.

"I'm not treating him badly," Aaron denied.

Sharona then put the news in perspective. "Look, that type of thing happens in Israel. The Middle East is a dangerous neighborhood. That is why every tour bus has a soldier on board with an Uzi. You can't be afraid to live your lives. That's what the terrorists want: to put fear in you so you cannot live freely. But we are tough; Israelis are sabras (like the fruit, sweet on the inside but thorny on the outside). You will have to tell the difference between an occasional bombing and the fact that we still can live a relatively peaceful life, because Israel is the homeland of the Jews. We deal with terrorists because we can. This is a difference between us and a country like Russia, where Jews are mistreated and are clamoring to flee."

"Sharona is right," Ezra agreed. "It's not as if every bus is going to be attacked. It's no different than the violent crime in the States. There are mass shootings every day, but you don't think twice about going outdoors, do you?"

Brent questioned, "If it's so safe, why do you have a soldier on the bus, on every bus?"

"It's a precaution," Sharona said, putting most at ease. "It's for security. It's defensive. We don't go looking for trouble, but in our own country, we have learned how to defend ourselves against our enemies."

Ahava reached for her guitar and tossed the strap over her head. She started to strum a little and Brent synchronized and played off her chords. The ambience of the bus resumed its harmony again as it rolled off toward our next site on the itinerary.

* * *

The bus drove us deep into the Negev desert where we hiked through canyons to rocky mountaintops, all along seeing different colored layers of rock, boulders, and natural rock formations that seemed to emulate sculptures. Not being avid hikers, Sharona warned us to wear hats against the brutal sunrays that could sap one's strength and cause dehydration within the hour. "Drink," Sharona harped. "Always drink from your canteen." She explained that dehydration could lead to dizziness and passing out. We didn't sweat much, because the air was dry and our perspiration evaporated quickly.

It was just a week ago that we were all wearing winter coats in the States. Now, we traversed in our hiking boots, shorts, and short-sleeved shirts under the shade of our caps. With our canteens and cameras dangling from our neck bands, we climbed over small boulders and stepped cautiously between them.

At one point near the top of a mountain, we needed to cross a stretch of rock that lay at a 90-degree angle. The only way across was to scooch on our rear ends, slowly stepping with our feet and hands in unison, inching our way across sharp burrs on the surface of the rocks that would surely shred our skin if we toppled over and rolled off the edge to our certain demise.

"Who thought of this? How is taking our life in our hands considered fun?" Diana bemoaned.

One of the overweight girls, Leah, let out a panicked scream and started to cry. But after a dramatic "rescue" from one of the guides, she sat whimpering to gather herself. It took her the longest to get to the other side and required a lot of coaxing and still one of the male guards helped her by hand overcome this treacherous part of the hike. Others such as Gabriel kept their fear in check, trying not to leak it in a recognizable facial expression. But he wasn't always successful as his eyes widened in a statement of terror. Daniel's eyes were hidden behind metallic sunglasses. But he suffered the same indignities of showing vulnerability too by cursing loudly during the challenge. This part of the mountain was like walking on our hands through shards of glass.

As we each took turns scooting across the 30 feet stretch of prickly incline with trepidation, we stood on a rocky plateau afterwards. Each of us examined our own hands and rubbed away at our reddened and bruised palms. As the group reassembled on the other side of the incline, we cheered on and coached the remaining members across the way until we were all safely on the other side.

We milled around talking and taking in the view of barren desert beyond the rocky mountainside. In a quiet moment, I stood staring off into the horizon, when Daniel came up from behind me and pushed me in the center of my spine, which thrust me toward the mountain edge.

The shock of the force from behind compounded exponentially at the threat of falling over to certain injury if not death. My heart seemed to stop as my arms flailed about and cartwheeled until I regained my balance short of the edge. I turned around and saw Daniel cackling at the fear he instilled through what he deemed a prank. Apparently, his machoism was necessary to combat his insecurities that leaked out during the scooching part of the trip. He was overcompensating.

We were mentally and physically exhausted. The group rested. Some lay under the sun on their backs. Others sat with their arms holding their folded knees, on which they rested their fatigued heads. Leah drank from her canteen and then offered it to anyone else. Hannah first took her up on it, wiping the opening with her shirt as if to magically dispel any germs, even though her shirt was soaking with sweat. She chugged some water and used her wrist to dry her mouth, then handed the canteen to yet another, Brent, who took it without any concern for germs and thrust it vertically and drank as rapidly as water could flow into his mouth. The fullest canteens were passed around until everyone replenished their bodily fluids.

We descended the mountain on the other side, so we didn't have to face the trepidatious part of the trip again. Each step had to be calculated to plant firmly on a flat surface of a substantial rock or else risk stepping in between rocks and twisting an ankle. Eventually we came back down and safely huddled at the bus. Hannah found solace in the arms of Gabriel, who unabashedly wrapped his brawny arms around his female companion as the first open bid for intimacy among us.

The day waned into the evening where we set up camp in the middle of the Negev desert. We encircled a campfire and ate food brought out from storage coolers on the bus. We cooked hot dogs over the fire and consumed a disproportionate amount of food typically eaten due to the thousands of calories we burned by hiking all day long over boulders under the desert sun.

Brent and Ahava brought out their guitars, flung the straps over their heads, and began playing songs for the rest of us. The evening became darker until only the campfire illuminated our faces. After the hot dogs were eaten, and the songs sung, and Sharona talked to us about what's to come in the following day, the campfire burned out and we retired to sleeping bags on the desert ground. With the light from the fire reduced to the glow of embers, we could see our shadows from the light of the moon and the billions of stars that splattered across the night sky canvas as if a Jackson Pollock painting. Against a midnight black sky, the tiny points of light were revealed in their true masses, unlike the skies of the city whose manufactured lights obscure the galaxy stars. Abigail reflected aloud a sentiment that we were all thinking: "We came halfway across the planet, and we're seeing the skies in their true beauty for the first time in our lives." Seeing the stars in their true amount, clarified to us all, atheists included, that the universe was mysterious, inexplicable, and magically beautiful but real.

We naturally awoke at sunrise and tried not to look at everyone to offer some sense of privacy. Some of the ladies walked away from camp a good distance to relieve themselves in nature, while some of the men simply went around to the other side of the bus and took a whiz.

Sharona imparted that we wouldn't be crossing into the Sinai Peninsula, because Israel had returned the land, which was captured in the famous Six-Day War. She explained in detail, "As you know, in 1967 there was a dispute over the Suez Canal when President Nasser of Egypt nationalized the canal, which was owned and operated by the British-French Suez Canal Company. So, Israel, France, and Britain invaded Egypt, Syria, and Jordan and captured the West Bank, the Golan Heights, the Gaza Strip, and the Sinai Peninsula all within a week. That is why it is called the Six-Day War. This land capture expanded the Israeli territory fourfold and provided not only room to grow, but served as a buffer zone and provided valuable water and mineral resources. Yet Israel has given back the Sinai and all its riches in exchange for a peace agreement with the Egyptians. Since the results of the war, Israel has been considered an elite military over its neighbors, especially in air superiority."

"I don't believe it… Israel was the aggressor?" Hannah said, miffed and in shock. "So, you're saying Israel started the war, won all this land, then gave it back?"

"Please settle down. Let me explain a little more," Sharona intervened. "The issue is more complicated than that. Israel did not initiate the war for material gain, even though that was the result of the war. The Egyptian President Nasser openly declared for the destruction of Israel and built up his armies, with Jordan and Syria, around Israel. The Israeli public was fearing existential annihilation, an imminent threat. So Israel launched a preemptive invasion. So technically, Israel shot the first bullet, but only because the Arab nations were preparing to pounce."

"But they pulled the trigger," Hannah qualified the technicality.

This time it was Sharona who responded with animation and disbelief of Hannah's naiveté, "What are they supposed to do, wait like sitting ducks for our country to be destroyed? You have to understand Israel is a tiny country. At its narrowest, it is only 9 miles wide. Once an enemy has the advantage of invading first, the rest of the country could collapse. When Israel goes to war, the fight for its very existence is the motivation. It doesn't go to war for glory or land acquisition, it fights for its right to be alive and free of danger. The Israelis don't target civilians; it is one of the most humane militaries in the world.

"There was a time before the state of Israel earned its foundational right to exist, that the military was nothing more than civilians with makeshift weapons. No fancy, high-tech jets or tanks, just basic artillery. The people were refugees and immigrants from Europe. But after the existence of the state was earned by a majority vote by the world leaders of the United Nations, we got the respect of our enemies by our sheer will to survive. Now our military and country have matured into a regional superpower, by necessity. Our pilots are revered like God himself. For they have proven invaluable to our defense and existence."

"That's what I'm going to be," Daniel declared boldly.

"You are going to join the Israeli Air Force?" Leah asked as if she was pleading him not to put himself in danger.

Ahava giggled, as if not taking him seriously.

"I'm serious. I'm going all the way in."

"You mean you want to 'make Aliyah'?" Ahava asked for clarification.

"What's that?" Gregory asked.

Sharona took over the explanation. "That's when someone Jewish or with Jewish ancestry migrates to Israel to live permanently and become an Israeli citizen. That's making Aliyah." Then in guide-like manner she added a history lesson to provide more background. "Most of the Jewish population migrated here from all over the world into one international melting pot. The Jews who settled in Germany and France during the Middle Ages are called Ashkenazi, while the Jews who were forced out of Spain after 1492 are called Sephardic Jews. They had fled to Eastern Europe and North Africa. But mostly Jews now live in either Israel or the United States, with only about a million in Europe, a few hundred thousand in South America, and about half that much in Russia. Roughly speaking of course. It's hard for the census to get accurate counts because of the usual reasons of people participating in the surveys and in defining who is Jewish."

Then Diana stepped into the conversation in a bellicose voice. "What do you mean by that? My parents are Jews, so I am."

Hannah then said, "By Jewish law, if the mother is Jewish, her children are Jewish, even if the father is not Jewish. Yet, the opposite is not the same. If the father is Jewish and has children with a non-Jew, then the children are not Jews."

Ezra chimed in and argued that point. "That's not true anymore. In 1983, an organization of Reform rabbis of some sort of Central Conference of American Rabbis passed a resolution that said 'the child of one Jewish parent is under the presumption of Jewish descent.'"

"So who are they to determine the status of who's who?" I said.

"They are legitimate Jewish leaders."

I decided to wrangle the subject with my buddy in an intellectual duel. "But not the only ones. The Reform Jews are the least religious. Of course, they will be liberal about it. But what do the Ultra-Orthodox have to say about it?"

"Oh right, because we are all Ultra-Orthodox Jews," he said sarcastically. "When was the last time you were even in a temple? Did you pray before eating breakfast this morning? Come on, we are all Reform Jews if not just secular all together.”

Diana boldly objected. “Both of my parents are Jewish, so I am too. But I don’t even believe or practice any of this nonsense.”

“Then why are you here?” I asked.

“To be honest,” Diana admitted, “I just canceled my engagement with my fiancé and wanted to get away from him as far as possible.”

The room went quiet with unspoken judgment that she was doing nothing more than running away from her personal problems, and didn’t carry an ideological torch to burn.

To break the awkward silence, I spoke up. “I am seeking a place where community is important, where everyone is like your brother and sister. I identify with being Jewish. That’s why I decided to come here and immerse myself in Judaic influences rather than go to Greece or Italy, or any other place.”

“Isaac, how can you consider yourself Jewish and not be committed to the rituals?” Brent asked.

“Same back at you,” I said. “You aren’t Hasidic, either. You choose the level of commitment you want. So what? My commitment is less visible than yours. Your commitment is less visible than a Conservative Jew or an Orthodox Jew. To each his own."

I followed up with another perspective. "D'you think any of our historical enemies would pardon any of us during the Spanish Inquisition or the Holocaust. They don't bother to differentiate whether you pray or not. They just slaughter."

"Well said," Ezra agreed.

Then Brent went on the offensive. "So you think our enemies determine your identity?"

Then running out of things to say, I finally rested on a simple notion. "I believe, if you think you're Jewish, then you are."

"That's a little flippant," Gabriel retorted. "Am I Greek Orthodox Christian simply if I think it?"

"If you thought it in earnest. But you don't, so you are just being argumentative," I replied now thinking I got in over my head and am just as naïve as anyone and not knowing definitively any of the answers.

As the reflective teens debated a centuries-old issue, our bus took off to the next destination. Our drowsiness gave way to intrigue as we peered out the windows at the near barren countryside, with little shrubbery teasing the landscape. This time we traveled to the western Negev. We stopped at a remote, flat area in the desert that seemed arbitrary, but soon we saw some pickup trucks and tents, and a few people dressed from head to toe in draping garbs. The women wore burkas. Their head coverings only revealed their mysterious eyes. We piled out of the bus and were greeted hospitably by the small clan we would come to know as Bedouins.

Sharona then explained, "The Bedouins are Arabic nomadic tribes that don't settle in any one area. They are peaceful and originated in Syria and later spread across northern Africa. They herd camels and goats, and although they dwell in the desert, they are not inhibited to embrace modern technology. You will see some of the men wearing watches."

A few camels were milling around the campsite. One of the Bedouins directed me to come. So, I approached the tall beast with a bit of concern. But then the nomad raised his arms in front of the gigantic animal and it obediently knelt to the desert floor and rested on its front and back legs, making his saddle align with the top of my head, but the stirrups were within reach. He motioned me to step into the stirrup, hoist myself up, and swing my other leg over the saddle until I was seated firmly on the mountainous back. Then the animal rose higher and higher as it stood from a kneeling position. He led the camel around for a few minutes as I kept my balance, hugging the beast's neck until feeling more confident to raise my back straight. I nervously smiled as Brent and Ahava and Ezra took photos of my grand appearance with each clop of the camel's hooves. After the camel returned to the campsite, the guide directed the animal to kneel. Once his belly met the desert floor, I gingerly slid off the side of the saddle and dismounted with a hop down. The nomadic guide held out his hand. Gabriel interjected, "Give him a few shekels."

"Oh, that's what he wants," I said feeling a bit snookered. I picked out a few bills and gave them to him.

Our group gathered around a small campfire with one of the nomadic women, named Fatima. She pancaked some sort of bread circle between her naked hands and cooked it over the fire on a hot rock along with a teakettle. After the water boiled, she poured it with tea grains in a shot glass and handed it to one of our group members. We were concerned about the sanitary conditions, but some of us sipped it out of courtesy while others just passed it along or feigned drinking to save face.

Diana's face turned off color and loudly raised her concern. "Is this sanitary?"

"I don't think there is a dishwasher in that tent," I quipped, which garnered snickers from the group.

After taking pictures and showing our appreciation, we piled back onto the bus and drove east. The journey lasted a couple of hours until we reached the Dead Sea.

Sharona captivated our attention once again by telling the story of the Dead Sea. "With its high salt and mineral content, we can float without fear of drowning. And the therapeutic properties are said to heal many ailments, such as acne, cuts, psoriasis, allergic reactions, and rheumatologic conditions. It's not just the salt; the minerals like magnesium and bromide reduce inflammation, stimulate blood circulation, and have other health benefits. This is not a myth. These are actual benefits from the sea."

With our bathing suits under our regular clothes, we got to the beach and removed our outer attire until we were just in our swimwear. Along with the others, I walked into the sea until the sea water reached my waist and then, as we were told to do, I lay back and let my legs rise to the surface. I wasn't even flat on my back. I floated effortlessly as if I were sitting in a bean bag with my legs bent and my buttocks submerged. My head lay fully above the surface. I wasn't expecting a miracle, but even with ample description ahead of time, the effortless buoyancy caused some new sensation of being in a strange and different place. We weren't in Kansas anymore.

Upon our return from magically floating upright in the sea, Sharona gathered us again to impart more history on the region. "The Dead Sea Scrolls are considered one of the most remarkable archaeological discoveries ever. They were found about when Israel first became an independent state and over the decades since then in 11 caves at the northwestern shore of the Dead Sea. The scrolls were written in about the 3rd century Before Common Era (BCE) through the 1st century of the Common Era (CE), but rather than scrolls as we know them to be, the Dead Sea Scrolls are actually a collection of about 25,000 fragments of papyrus, leather, and copper that range from a few feet to the size of a fingernail. They were written a thousand years before the earliest known records to date of similar biblical references. Later in the week, we will see the actual scrolls, which are on display in a Jerusalem museum."

* * *

The following day, the group traveled to the outskirts of Jerusalem. Sharona used the microphone to get everyone's attention and began her introduction to our next adventure.

"Jebusites were Canaanites who lived in a strong fortressed city called Jebus, which is disputed by scholars, but is, by one camp, believed to be the foundation of Jerusalem. From biblical references, King David conquered the Jebusite city of Jebus around 1003 BCE by a remarkable strategy. One of his men climbed through a water shaft and entered the city inside its walls. He then ran across the compound unnoticed by the Jebusite army and opened the front gates, which enabled King David's army to invade and conquer the city. You are about to enter the ancient waterway and experience it for yourselves."

Wearing street clothes and sandals, we cautiously stepped into a hole in the side of the rocky wall. We walked a few steps and plunged into cold water. Finding our footing on the uneven floor of the cavity, we yelped, complaining that our clothes were submerged to our waists. "Hold onto the person in front of you for safety," Sharona bellowed. "Soon as we walk a little farther the canal will be pitch dark." We ambled along in centipede fashion in the underground blackness, thrusting our feet through a wall of water. With the bed of the canal irregularly snaking left, right, up, and down, our footing was challenged and progression slowed.

We reached a point where the shaft changed from mostly lateral to vertical. Sharona turned on a flashlight to illuminate the rocky wall before us. "This is where the brave soldier is thought to have climbed to enter the inner walled city of Jebus." She further explained, "When the waterway was discovered and excavated by archaeologists, it challenged us to think how such a waterway could have been constructed in ancient times without the use of modern instruments to guide their chiseling through solid rock." After a while Sharona volunteered the answer. "Originally, it is believed, workmen started chiseling through the rock at both ends and when they got close to one another, they yelled, which could be heard through the divide. They chiseled toward each other's hollers that could be heard more easily the closer the two work parties got to each other until the connection was made. That is why the canal is so uneven."

Ahava was in front of me, so naturally my hand rested on her shoulder just as the person behind me rested his hand on mine as we sloshed through the water in the pitch-black darkness. I couldn't help but feel the warmth of her body and fantasize about being with her in a more intimate way. Our feet groped the bed of the waterway feeling for sudden steplike rises or falls as we turned around to go back. Gregory lost his footing, along with his camera, which submerged below the water's surface when he fell. He cursed and accused Daniel, who was behind him, of pushing him. "You're paying for that," Gregory screamed out.

Daniel denied it completely, "I didn't do anything to you, idiot. You tripped on your own."

We slogged a quarter mile back to the entrance until the outside sunshine guided us in our final steps into the light of day.

At the hotel, we washed and changed clothing. After a rest, we milled about visiting each other's rooms and conversing about the sites we had seen thus far. "It has been a lot more physical than I thought. I'm exhausted," Ahava admitted.

Ahava and Ezra were lying in the same bed but on opposite ends with their feet overlapping in the middle. We were all getting more and more comfortable with each other. I sat leaning my chest on the backside of a chair concealing my inner anxieties of their proximity to each other. I then said, "We're going to have a big day tomorrow seeing Jerusalem in detail. First, we go to the Old City to see the markets, the Dome of the Rock, and of course, the Western Wall. That's a lot in one day. It will take some time to get up close to some of the sites because of the lines." We talked about our experiences so far and what we hoped to get out of the trip.

Steve entered the room with Abigail and Hannah. Homelife back in the States was blasé for most of us, except Steve, who had a girlfriend with whom he had to part. In what sounded like a confessional, Steve said in his slow speech, "We just started seeing each other and wham, I'm off across the world. I'd do anything to be with her. I'm just sick to my stomach being so far away and for so long. I'm homesick already."

I offered a contrary view. "I'm not. Just the opposite, I couldn't stand being at home listening to my parents nag all the time about my schoolwork and so forth. I couldn't breathe without some sort of derisive criticism. As far as I'm concerned, the hell with it. I'm finding a new place without parental domination."

"Well, you couldn't be farther away at this point," Ezra said.

"Hey, whatever, I'm here to experience the here and now. I left my past behind me on the tarmac at LaGuardia," I said.

Gabriel entered the hotel room wearing just pants. Barefoot and shirtless, he nonchalantly walked in the room where three beds lay, and sat on an unoccupied mattress. "What's going on?" he asked.

"Just jibber jabbering about homelife," I summed up.

"Homesick already, we've only been away about a week." Gabriel expressed his incredulity.

"I have a girlfriend back in Ohio. I really didn't want to leave her. We were just getting serious," Steve said as if sleep deprived.

"Well, this is the trip of a lifetime," Gabriel said, then challenged, "In what other time in your life will you get the chance to take 6 months off and not work, not study, and just explore and discover your true self?"

"But we will be working and studying Hebrew later in the trip. I really don't think this trip is for me," Steve admitted.

"You're just lovesick," I said.

"She really means a lot to me. I don't think it's anything else."

"Simplifying it, Steve, you are horny and you value sex more than this adventure." I put it out on the table.

"She's really the one I want to be with right now. Excuse me, I have to make a phone call."

After Steve left the room, Ezra stated, "I wouldn't be surprised if Steve goes home early; he seems to lack any kind of conviction or even curiosity about Israel."

"Why come all the way over here to turn around and go home after a week just for a relationship," said Gabriel. "That's crazy."

"That's the pull of sex on a 17-year-old," I tried to impress upon my peers. "We're all at that point in our lives, but I would like to think we are all more sophisticated than just horn-dogs."

"He must not be very interested in Judaism," Ezra said.

"Are any of us? Are we here for exploration and adventure or to become more religious?" I asked.

"It's different for each of us I think," Ezra reflected.

"I'm in it to simply bask in my autonomy and explore the freedoms I have now without the restrictions of collegiate exams and parents," I admitted.

"I'm here to deepen my relationship with God and Judaism," Brent spoke up.

"Well, aren't you serious? I don't believe in God as the concept is depicted by humankind. It's beyond human comprehension, so why bother?" Ahava said.

Abigail spoke up. "I'm here because my parents thought I would mature being away from home. I guess I'm a momma's baby. I am really missing her. She's my best friend."

"So you didn't take this trip through your own initiative?" I asked.

"I take Judaism seriously. My entire family is secular, but I've always appreciated my Jewish heritage and want to build on what I already know. When I return to the States, I'm going to major in Judaic studies," she elaborated.

"What are you going to do with a degree in that?" Ezra asked.

"There's a lot here in Israel where a degree in Judaic studies is applicable to various aspects of the society."

"Yeah? Like what, being a tour guide?" I pressed her.

"Actually, I'm thinking of enrolling in rabbinical school after college. I may even do that in Israel. I already know how to speak a little Hebrew. I'm in the intermediate range. I just have to perfect it and become somewhat fluent. That's why I'm really here. So I can learn Hebrew better and practice it in the streets. Every day is like being in a saturated lab of Hebrew speakers."

"You are really serious then. You think you're going to make Aliyah?" Ezra probed.

"We'll see. I do miss my mom."

"You know, Abigail, if you make Aliyah, you will be separated from your nuclear family by five thousand miles," Ezra calculated.

"Yeah, I know, but my mission in life is personal and goes beyond my immediate comforts. Besides, I can return to the States every so often for annual visits, and they can visit me sometime. It's really no different than if I were to live in California while they reside in New York."

"What about the army?" David questioned. "You'll have to serve a mandatory term, like a two-year stint if you really want to be accepted by Israeli society. They just won't accept you based on a sacrifice of leaving your home to come here. Just about every Israeli has lost a family member to war. You will always be an outsider, especially because you're American."

"Why do you say that?"

"Because, don't you feel the resentment Israelis have towards American Jews?" he said knowingly.

Abigail tried to argue the point, but only put forth a superficial aspect. "Americans are always giving money to Israel to both the government and Israeli Jews."

"And they resent having to be coddled," Ezra clarified. "They take pride in being an independent state, not a puppet of the great United States. And the common Israeli resents having to risk their blood by being here defending the Jewish homeland and its principles and living on the fringe of poverty. Suffering with sky-high inflation while American Jews relax and get rich. It's envy and resentment. Besides, they have seen their fill of Jewish Americans trying to make Aliyah over the years. They come with great ideals, but leave after a few years, missing and eventually returning to the easy life in America."

"They have a point, though," I said. "They are sacrificing their blood and dealing with enemies that surround them for their sake and the sake of Jews all over the world."

"What are American Jews supposed to do, give up their good life and turn their backs on their families?" Gabriel posed.

"They say bring your families with you," David added.

"Yeah, like that's feasible," Gabriel said, "when most of my family doesn't even think of Israel. I'm the only one in my family who is passionate about moving to Israel. Besides, who am I, the family dictator who tells the rest of my family where to live? My father has worked for the US government for the past 20 years. My mother has a business with clientele tied to the area. They aren't going to abruptly or any other way leave their careers and way of life, just because their teenage son wants them to."

"They like the good life. Ha," Brent said.

"It's not just the good life. While they raised us with Jewish schooling in a Conservative synagogue, and went every Saturday for services, we didn't really practice the rituals at home. Just Passover and Hanukkah. You know, for the high holidays, we went to the synagogue for a most monotonous experience," Gabriel said.

"I wouldn't exactly consider Hanukkah a high holiday," Ezra argued more proficiently. "Rosh Ha Shannah, the new year; Yom Kippur, the praying for our sins; and Passover, the freedom from slavery: those are high holidays. Hanukkah is just a minor military-related story of a so-called miracle that some Jews survived for eight days on one day's supply of oil. But only in the US is it a big deal among Jews. And it came this way because of the overwhelming powerful influence Christmas has on the young. The Jewish parents don't want their kids to feel left out of gift giving and celebrations, so Hanukkah came to assume the same commercial qualities as Christmas has over the years, since they both occur around the same time of the year. But in Israel, they don't give too much weight on that holiday. Can you even spell Hanukkah?"

Then David interjected. "Yeah, it's C-h-a-n-u-k-a-h," he spelled confidently.

"See there is not even consensus on how to spell it." Ezra made his point. "That's a microcosm that exemplifies what is so messed up about organized religion. The rabbis speak in Hebrew, and we don't know what the hell is going on. But we're expected to go through all these rituals and pray in Hebrew. Between the schism of Science and Religion, and the demanding rituals, and the lack of understanding, it's just not appealing to the masses."

"Well, you know, you can be Jewish without being religious. There're all kinds of denominations and types of Jewish identity," Brent said.

"Like what?" Ahava asked.

"Well, you know about the Hassidic Ultra-Orthodox, who dedicate their entire days to prayer and ritual, the Orthodox, who do the same but also work in the real world; then come the Conservative group, who don't quite follow all of the scripture rituals thoroughly. They're a little more pragmatic, but very committed religiously. The Reform Jews tend to dilute the rituals and prayer to the basics and tend to want to do everything in a modern language such as English. But did you know about Reconstructionists? Observant, Humanists, and Cultural Jews?"

"Tell me more, Rabbi Brent," David teased.

"Very funny," Brent replied, not getting too offended by his younger cohort.

"Did you know like three-quarters of Israeli Jews are secular? Nonbelievers in God as depicted in the Bible. They don't observe the traditions, rituals, or religious practices. But they consider themselves Jewish because they live here," Ezra tried to clarify.

"So where are we going with all these divisions?" Gabriel questioned. "The things we have in common are just as pronounced: we share a history of one of the world's original philosophies on monodeities. We share a common language: Hebrew. We share ancestral history that originates to the beginning of civilization. And most important, we rejoice in spite of our neighbors breeding hatred."

"Despite being chased out of Europe, Jews have thrived both in the diaspora and in the resurrection of our homeland: Israel. We proudly live, work, pray, and value life: La Chaim!" (to life!)

And for the first time on the trip, I noticed we all transitioned to referring to Israel using the possessive "our," as in "our homeland."

* * *

Being a minority among the group of believers, I was drawn closer to Ahava who shared the same disdain for organized religion, but proudly identified with being Jewish. We took a walk from our hotel and strolled through the streets of Jerusalem. I wanted to hold Ahava's hand while we walked, but thought it too pretentious. So, when is it right to push behavior to the next level of intimacy? She's talked to just about everybody in the group as if a bee pollinating flowers. Why should I think she is into me any more than anyone else? I thought.

"We still have the night life to experience," I said. "Come on, we are in Jerusalem, the nerve center of three great religions and more."

Yet here we were alone together milling about the streets of Jerusalem at night. The streets were congested with cars honking about, the sidewalks jammed with pedestrians, many of whom were tourists from all over, especially Europe.

"Look, the sign says 'American Ice Cream,'" Ahava noticed.

"Yeah," I said, "they figure if they put 'American' in front of anything, it will sell better. While they quietly despise feeling inferior and dependent on America, they sure do want anything American, whether it be TVs or the latest gadgetry. They feel they should live just as well as Americans."

"That's so bizarre. I'm American but don't care about any of that stuff or appearance. I'm a minimalist. I wear the same jeans for years," she said.

We saw a jewelry shop. "This is the one that Sharona recommended." I went in and saw an array of gold, silver, and diamond jewelry. "Ahava," I said with a lump in my throat, "you are going to think I'm the biggest hypocrite right about now."

"Why, Isaac?"

"I'm not into material possessions, per se, but it would be nice to get a tchotchke to remember this trip," I told her.

"Really? That's all you're worried about. Get what you want. You don't have to prove anything like you don't need material things to make you happy. I can see these things as just mementos and guilty pleasures."

"Thanks," I said.

"You don't need my approval," she said.

"I know I don't need your approval. I just don't want to come across as a hypocrite."

"Everyone is," she said cynically, yet jokingly.

I asked the shop owner, "Can I see the 'Chai,' the Hebrew letters that mean life, please?" I held the glistening gold Hebrew letters and chain in my hand and could see my mirrored reflection from the face of the necklace. "Is this real gold?" I asked trying to avoid getting ripped off but feel foolish to rely on the seller to validate its authenticity.

"Yes, 14k," he said sternly.

"How much do you want for it?"

"I can do 50 US dollars for you, my friend."

"How do I know it's real gold?"

"It is real, it is 14k gold," he insisted, getting a little perturbed at my mistrust.

Still incredulous due to a naiveté in such matters, I asked, "Does that mean it's solid gold?" as if more simple questions would reveal a truth that could only be obtained by asking the same questions repeatedly.

"No," the old man said definitively shaking his head. "If it were solid gold, it would be too soft. 14k gold is the standard for this type of jewelry. What you don't want is gold-plated," the old Jeweler stated in a reassuring and patient manner until he closed the deal.

Still with uncertainty lingering, I took a gamble, since it glistened under the bright lights, and with a reluctancy said, "All right then, I guess I'll take it."

At that, the old man behind the counter, agreed to $50 and quickly wrapped the piece in a small box and bag, then handed it to me in exchange for the American currency. It's pretty cool, I thought, then proclaimed, "Now people will know I'm Jewish."

Ahava shot back, "I think your jet black, curly hair and fair complexion give that away."

"Yeah, I don't know why we talk about all the denominations all the time when we can spot a Jew in crowd just by their features. Seems like Jewishness is more of a race than anything else," I proclaimed as if I said an obvious truth.

"What about converts?" Ahava challenged.

"You got me there."

"What about the Jews who come from South America or Asia, or Africa?" She continued to dismantle my perception.

"Well, they probably came from the Middle East or Europe first," I said, trying to salvage my theory.

"I know you are excited about talking about everything Jewish, since we're here in Jerusalem and all, but really, we can talk about other things, can't we?" she begged.

I took the opportunity to inquire about her feelings toward the group members. "Can you tell me whether you like anybody from the group a whole lot?" I inquired.

"I like just about everyone," she said without getting pinned down.

Now I sounded as if I was begging. "I mean, are you romantically interested in anyone in particular?"

She laughed. "Not at the moment. No."

"Not even Ezra?"

"I like Ezra. We have a connection. But I'm not so sure it's more than an infatuation."

"What about Gabriel?"

"He's okay. But he's a ladies' man. He will go through life always tempted to stray."

"David?"

"Too young and a little too radical for me."

"Radical?"

"Yeah, every time he talks, it's about stopping corruption in the government. He's going to grow up to be a rebel of some sort."

"I don't know about that. David has a healthy intellect and comes from a rich home. Besides, he too is a vegetarian who wouldn't hurt an ant. What about me?"

"Oh, Isaac, you are the sweetest, but we really don't know each other, now do we?"

"I-I- know that. I'm just seeing. You know, whether you like anybody. You know, so far."

"Well, I do, but probably not in the same way you are thinking," she said with caressing words. We seemed to have gently danced around embarrassment and humiliation. "So you like being here in Israel?"

"What's not to like, it's 78 degrees at night in the middle of winter. I'm walking with a beautiful woman in the most famous city on Earth."

Ahava scoffed at the compliment, then said, "I can't wait to explore Jerusalem in the daylight tomorrow."

"I think we're going to see the Dead Sea Scrolls, or remnants of some kind. Then we go to the Old City to see the Dome of the Rock and the Western Wall. Then we go to Yad Vashem. But for now, I'm hungry. Are you, Ahava?"

"I could eat something."

In our meanderings through Jerusalem, we came across an interesting place to eat called "Tea & Pie." We walked in. People were smoking and lying along the perimeter of the room on the floor. The few tables were also full. The cook came out and told people at a table to move closer together so the two tourists could sit. We ordered mushroom and cheese crepes, and felt as one with the nationals.

* * *

The following morning, we awoke and ate our continental breakfast of pastries and coffee. "This is all we get?" Brent bellyached. "When they said 'continental' breakfast, I was thinking a huge smorgasbord, not some dainty muffin and coffee."

Gabriel then sounded annoyed and said, "Now you have graduated to a sophisticated world traveler."

Sharona entered the breakfast room of the hotel and waited for everyone to settle in before introducing the day's itinerary. "First, we go to one of the holiest places of worship and pilgrimage to the Jewish people, the Western Wall on the Temple Mount in the Old City. The Western Wall is the only remains of the great Second Temple of King Herod after the Romans destroyed the temple in 70 CE. Actually, it is not the second temple itself but a retaining wall. But this is what is left of an era when Jews last enjoyed self-rulership… That was two thousand years ago. The Old City is divided in four unequal parts: The Armenian Quarter, the Jewish Quarter, the Muslim Quarter, and the Christian Quarter. The Muslim Quarter is the largest in size and population."

The group boarded the bus that took us to the Old City. We walked into the Jewish Quarter and to an open square area. At first, we saw the expansive open area where hordes of tourists, in casual clothing and with cameras hanging from their shoulder straps, mixed with Hassidim praying at the great Wall, which was made of 5-feet high, square stones, each weighing tons. Numerous Hassidim, in black garb and wearing flat hats, stood in front of the Western Wall with nothing between them and the Wall except their Bible from which they recited prayers. They rhythmically bowed as they prayed.

Sharona continued her overview at the Wall. "The tourists write messages and prayers on slips of paper, fold them, and insert them in a crevice between the stones of the Western Wall in the hopes and belief that their prayers will be answered. At the end of the evening, many of the prayers fall out and drop to the ground where maintenance crews sweep them up and bury them in the Mount of Olives, according to tradition.

"In several spots among the stones, weeds grew from the crevices and accented the otherwise tall wall that stretches about 200 feet long and stands about 62 feet high.

"It used to be called the 'Wailing Wall' because when the lands were governed by the Romans between 324 and 638 AD, the Jews wept and lamented at the destruction of their two temples.

Exacerbating the Jewish misery were the Muslims who, during their 1,000-year rule of the area, used the Jewish prayer site as a garbage repository to humiliate the Jews. Prayer at the Wall was permitted under British rule of the region and became popular by the late 19th century. However, despite an armistice allowing Jews to visit the Wall, the Jordanians ruled the area from 1948 to 1967 and did not allow Jewish access to the Wall. It was only when the Israelis captured the West Bank including the Old City during the Six-Day War that Jews resumed their ritual prayers at the site. The Western Wall is considered the holiest place Jews can pray."

I wrote a message on a note—something about world peace—folded it, and stuck it in a gap between two stones, an action Ahava noticed.

"Why did you do that?" She called me out.

Trying to justify my actions as "normal," I replied, "It's what people do."

"You don't honestly believe whatever you wrote will come true, do you?"

"Look, I just wanted to participate in the ritual."

She dismissively walked away. I caught up to her. "I'm not saying I believe in superstition, but like if you disdain Judaism so much, why did you bother to come all this way?"

Ahava didn't have all the answers, but she always had an answer. "Sometimes, I feel Jewish; sometimes not. I just don't believe. Alright, it's so stupid."

"I don't believe either, but being Jewish is more than beliefs and more than ritual."

"I'm listening."

"We're a society linked together no matter what our denominations are, or our geographical distances, or our level of knowledge of the traditions, but you know, we define ourselves and our enemies define us as well. And throughout history, our enemies, whether it be the Egyptians, Romans, Spaniards, Muslims, Ottomans, or Germans, we resist against them as a unified people."

"Why can't people just be regular, like? Why do we need this identity?" she pleaded in exasperation.

"Because the world is fragmented in independent cultures, some of which will target us whether we accept or reject our identity. Look, if Hitler is calling you a Jew and trying to destroy you, regardless of what your self-perception is, you best run, escape, fight back, or that will be the end of you, Ahava."

"But that's all in the past, Isaac."

"There's plenty of antisemitism all over the world including in the US, now. For some, hatred is an ideology that never dies out completely. Human nature hasn't changed over the millennia. Bigotry and antisemitism continue to this day."

"Why can't the world just be secular?"

"Well, that's the trend, but religion has a stranglehold on those who want simple answers. And there is an endless supply of people who are groomed from birth to believe in deities that lord over our daily decisions and actions."

"So why do you bother sticking in a prayer on a piece of paper between the rocks as if it will have some sort of tangible result?"

"I don't know, I just like participating so I get a feeling. By ignoring the rituals, you are like going to an amusement park and never riding a roller coaster. Until you actually do ride one, you can only hypothesize what it feels like."

"You are mixing me all up."

"I don't know. I'm just saying I want to get to know what others do and feel by going through the motions like they do."

"So it's amusement to you? You imitate what you see and think you can feel what a religious person feels. I don't think it works that way." Ahava put it on the line.

"How do you know?" I said almost in retaliation.

"What you don't understand," she explained, "is that a religious person perceives their relationship with God as a tangible, real thing that can be felt and communicated with."

"I get it," I replied. "They react viscerally and feel physically associated with the inanimate concept of God. Look, you and I are in the same Humanist sector. Maybe you're right, by mimicking a religious person's actions, I will do nothing more than amuse myself. I will never be able to understand their paradigm and feel what they feel. So why am I here? Despite being secular, all that we are seeing now in Israel is real history. Whether I am into Judaism or not, it's our heritage, and identity."

Ahava then grabbed my arm. "Come on, let's walk through all the quarters of the Old City."

* * *

At the entrance of the Muslim Quarter, an Arab man in white garb made long, skinny loaves of bread over a firepit, attending to each loaf like a tailgater at a football game tending to a hot dog on the grill.

Ahava and I walked along a sloping corridor of uneven steps made of stone slabs, their edges worn down to the nub by centuries of traversing by the Old City's inhabitants. The natives wore thobes and head coverings. On the right and left, vendors of all types of goods aligned the corridor: clothing, shoes, food. One vendor sold raw lamb hides, which was suspended from the ceiling of his tiny space. Hundreds of black flies covered the naked beasts. Seeing that, our stomachs churned viscerally, but we walked on through the shock.

"Who would eat that?" Ahava choked out her concern.

"This is their market," I said more accepting, then tried to put a perspective to it. "It's no different than going to Safeway."

"I think there's a little difference, don't you think? You know, packaging and freshness," she said.

"You know what I mean," I backtracked.

"No, not really. This is truly different," she said excitedly. "Like in worlds apart different."

As we descended the wide stone slabs serving as stairs below our feet, an old decrepit man walked with a wooden makeshift cane. His back bent into a humping curve, with his head seemingly stemming from his stomach. He shuffled in scabbed bare feet toward us. His face was so weathered and worn, only his few remaining teeth were visible. He stopped, and retched several times and spat with no regard to anyone. A glob of green phlegm projectiled from his mouth and puddled in the middle of the stone step where the indigenous residents and tourists trespass up and down. The old, anonymous man hocked once more and spat again as if making his mark on a world that otherwise dismissed him.

Then a bevy of Arabic children clamored to our side, screaming, "Two sheklim. Two sheklim," while thrusting a hand full of postcards close to our faces. They competed with each other to sell us these postcards. We were white Westerners in bright t-shirts and blue jeans. We stood out and were surrounded by shirtless children who swarmed us as if they were hordes of flies on a raw lamb hide.

We exited from the commercial section of the walled-in city and caught up with the group and Sharona. To our left and right were stone walls interrupted by a door or window. It was clean and where inhabitants lived. We walked through the four unequal quarters: the Christian, Muslim, Armenian, and Jewish Quarters. Then Sharona elaborated, "The Temple Mount is home to the Dome of the Rock, a golden structure with a mysterious inside where Muslims pray, pilgrimage, and believe Muhammed took his night journey from the rock beneath the Golden Dome. Muslims believe the Domed Rock is where God created the world. It is the Muslims' oldest surviving architectural structure and was built about 691 CE."

After a while, immersed in this other world where some 36,000 Muslims, Jews, Christians, and Armenians reside, we exited to modernity outside the walled Old City. Blaring horns and other traffic noise of the modern city struck our senses first, together with exhaust fumes from passing buses and rumbling trucks. Ahava and I broke away from the group again in search of a falafel stand, which were commonly available throughout the city. We walked along a sidewalk and came across one that looked clean. The clerk scooped a collection of fried chickpea balls and stuffed them into an opened pita bread. Cucumbers, sliced cherry tomatoes, and onions topped with tzatziki sauce covered the open end of the sandwich. We bit into our sandwiches and savored the Mediterranean flavors until our bellies were full. "This is really good, but I wonder how often these street vendors change their cooking oils," she said.

"It's a problem for some, you just have to go to a reputable one," I said. "It's a problem no matter where you are, even in the US. They all try to cut expenses by cutting corners."

I felt a deep emotional attachment to Ahava, which was accented by romantic gestures that fell short of anything beyond friendship. That was the frustrating and confusing part. She would throw her arms around me and squeeze tightly so that my arms were pinioned inside hers, which made it impossible for me to reciprocate the affection. She always took the initiative to make physical contact. She seemed untouchable, as if touching her is inherently prohibited by scripture. She made her move only when we were at a standstill in communication. She would probe for a deeper understanding of my emotions, and having no ability to articulate a feeling, I sat and stared out into the horizon. At this impasse, she thrust her arms around me, and that was it.

* * *

While we finished eating our falafel, we continued walking through the streets of Jerusalem and getting a deeper understanding of each other.

I finally just asked the obvious question everyone our age grapples with. "What are you going to do with your life?"

"I'm interested in a career in music," she stated unequivocally.

"Can you make a living doing that?"

"It's the only thing that makes me really, really happy."

"But don't you think it would be hard to make a living in music?"

"I come from a well-endowed family. My father works for the Nuclear Regulatory Commission and has a pretty high-level executive position. We have an agreement that he would support me financially if I needed it so long as I graduate from college. But who knows, I may be married after I finish college. Even so, I don't really think about financial survival much. The universe will provide."

"Or at least Daddy will."

"Hey," she said, somewhat offended by the implied criticism.

Feeling like a heel, I immediately apologized. "Sorry, Ahava. I guess it's different for fellas." I swallowed, thinking I just put my sandaled foot in my mouth again implying that life is harder for men than for women. Then in an effort to save face, I angled the discussion to a new subject. "Do you get along with your parents?"

"More or less. We don't always see eye to eye, and I'm very strong willed. What about you and your family?"

"I don't have much to do with them," I said. "They both work and I went to school and worked, so it's like our paths haven't crossed too much since I started working at 14. That's how I was able to do what I wanted. I have saved enough money for this trip and so they couldn't object much more than in a cosmetic way. I basically told them I was going. That I needed to explore the world a bit and do it on my own. They went along with my plan, so long as I did it formally through an organized group. I figured that would be better anyway. That way everything is coordinated for me, place to stay, places to see, transportation, food. All taken care of. So it was done, but they weren't about to pay for my ambitions to travel. I assumed that financial obligation, but like I said, I've saved a lot over the years I've been working."

"Where was that?"

"Just jobs that gave me an opportunity to work. You know, car washes at first, then pizza restaurants as a short-order cook and dishwasher, and a clerk in a bookstore."

"Oh. Cool. Which one?"

"It was one of the first discount bookstores. Crown."

"I'm reading this book that I think you will like. But it's hard to read in spots."

"Yeah?"

"It's *The Zen Artist*."

"Artist, huh. I declared my major in art, but I'm thinking of changing it to English when I return home."

"Why?"

"I just don't think I can make a good living in art."

"So what are you going to do?"

"I think anything else would work out better. I can always do art on my leisure time. Right?"

"I guess it depends how passionate you are with it. Music for me is my soul. So for me it's that or nothing. Maybe you have a different level of intensity with your association with art."

"Maybe. I don't know. I don't know what the future will be like. Other than I suppose I will continue my college studies and finish, you know, get a degree so I can get a decent job. You know, beyond dishwasher or bookstore clerk."

"Have you thought about transferring to Haifa University here in Israel?"

"Yeah, well, not really. Academics are hard enough in English. I would think it 10 times harder in a foreign language I don't competently speak."

"But we will learn Hebrew when we start the Ulpan next week, when we move in with our new Israeli families."

"That's only a 3-month program, though. I don't think we will become fluent speakers within that short time."

"I already know a smattering of Hebrew," she said, "and we can use it every day here in Jerusalem."

"We'll see." I wanted to kiss her so badly. But our conversation was going along and I didn't want to abruptly short-circuit it. At least we were getting to know each other in private, where my presence was not diluted with others chiming in. I felt connected to Ahava emotionally. She was a free spirit, a happy-go-lucky, unburdened by the kinds of problems I brought about myself: isolation, self-criticism, unknowing of a clear path forward. Ahava gregariously interacted with people. She flowed through society as if she were a brook through a forest, nourishing it. Nothing could contain her. She splashed her contagious laughter everywhere and with everyone, yet here I sat with Ahava at my side flashing looks into each other's eyes, causing our hearts to skip a beat throughout our conversation.

We stopped at a store that sold sandals and browsed through the merchandise. The clerk listened to the radio as was common among the Israelis so they could always hear the news. The announcer on the radio then stated, *"A Katusha rocket was launched from Gaza and fell into the nearby town of Sderot."* After hearing that bit of news, Ahava asked, "Why are they bombing a town that is integrated with Arab and Jews? Aren't the militants concerned about their own kind?"

I offered my view the best I understood the politics of the region. "They cause terror anywhere in Israel. Old women are strapped with explosives and walk into a crowded market and detonate the bomb to obliterate everyone around them including themselves. They don't care about any consequences except maximum terror and the ultimate destruction of Israel. If the Palestinians would embrace peace and elect non-terroristic leaders, then you would see the Gaza Strip receive an overwhelming amount of wealth given by the rest of the world that would pour in and improve the lives of the citizens. Instead, they smuggle in weapons and dig tunnels to invade Israel. The only way for the Israelis to prevent more carnage is to blow up the tunnels and blockade the Gaza Strip, which causes hardship on the inhabitants."

"Will we be within range of their missiles?" she asked.

"Probably not. We will be in the major cities: Beersheva, Tel Aviv, Haifa, and Jerusalem. While the Hezbollah have targeted Tel Aviv, most of their missiles have been intercepted by the Iron Dome Defense System, which was the only effective defense Israel had against hundreds of missiles directed toward civilian populations."

"So why do the citizens of Gaza elect terrorists for leaders?" she explored.

"The Hezbollah and other terrorist groups have financial backing by Iran. The citizens of Gaza don't have a lot of choices. The people with the money are the terrorist groups. They are the most visible and the most ruthless against any political opposition."

I walked Ahava back to the hotel and called it a night. But my thoughts of her penetrated my mind in an obsessive and possessive manner. She is perfect,

I thought. We are connected. I imagined her sharing my bed and holding her tightly through the early morning. But we did no such act. She simply walked to her room shared by three other female group members, and I to my room shared by three male group members.

* * *

The next morning, Ezra asked me how it went with Ahava. "We had a good time," I said and left that reply up to his interpretation. We piled into the bus after our quickly consumed continental breakfast. And we were driven to the Israel Museum to see up close the Dead Sea Scrolls.

We peered through a glass barrier between us and the 2,300-year-old manuscripts found west of the Dead Sea shores in 11 caves. The scrolls were brittle, which caused scholars to painstakingly piece fragments back together over the past 70 years so they could be legible again. Some larger portions of intact parchment and papyrus displayed for many feet showing off the Hebrew, Aramaic, and Greek text. Altogether, scholars reconstructed about 950 manuscripts.

"It's quite an archaeological find. It's as if I could envision the scribes of the third century BCE writing on the parchment," Sharona lectured.

In the swift changes of environment from site to site, it was easy to confuse where and what would be seen next, until someone asked what was next on the itinerary. Sharona simply replied, "Yad Vashem." And with many on the bus giving her a blank look, she explained, "The living museum and memorial for the Holocaust."

The group entered the museum with the momentum of enthusiasm that had been with us from the inception of the trip. Why not, it's another part of Israel and a significant happening of our shared heritage.

Hours later, we exited Yad Vashem in a stupor, stunned into submission from the horrific film footage taken by the Nazis of their own atrocities, showing hundreds of Jews digging their own mass grave before standing naked in the pit and being fired upon by machine gun until they all lay atop each other cheated out of life.

Jews were carried off in trucks to a remote area of the woods, told to disembark, line up, remove their clothes, and stand still. They were executed by a firing squad. Single bullets were cheaper than machine-gun ammunition.

In a more sinister, cost-effective killing approach, Jews were corralled into trucks by viciously barking German shepherds, only to soon realize, the exhaust fumes were being funneled back into the truck, killing the Jews while simultaneously being transported to dumping grounds where bulldozers pushed mountains of mangled bodies into the nameless, mass graves. After the bodies were buried, the earth covered them, leaving no visible trace of human existence.

At the height of Hitler's systematic extermination, Jews walked in long lines to enter shower rooms at death camps such as Chełmno, Belzec, Sobibor, Treblinka, Majdanek, and Auschwitz-Birkenau, only to die at the release of toxic gas. The screams didn't last long as dozens in the shower room fell to the floor with their last gasp of life learning the truth. The Nazis disposed of the dead bodies by putting them into ovens that burned the flesh and bones into ashes.

Back in the bus, the ride back to the hotel was eerily silent as we were all deeply contemplative. This is what happens when people don't get organized and fight for their basic dignities and freedom. This is why the Jews need a homeland. The Nazis rose to power within a technologically advanced democratic country not much different from the United States. It could happen anywhere.

Ezra took the lead to verbalize what we were all reflecting. "Just look at the rise of neo-Nazis, fanatic cult followers, paramilitant white supremacists, and others thinking and planning to overthrow the government or start a civil war, in America. They have deluded themselves into believing in unsubstantiated conspiracy theories and disinformation. What do I take away from all this? People in any society are gullible, suggestable, and fearful. And some leaders exploit all those qualities."

"Then why remain Jewish, if all it brings is trouble?" Gabriel questioned.

"Trouble isn't limited to just the Jews," Ezra explained. "In addition to the six million Jews murdered by the Nazis, there were millions of others who shared the same fate: Poles, Blacks, the disabled, Gypsies, LGBTQ+ persons, and anyone who was against the Third Reich. And that's just during World War II. Genocides occur all over the world to populations who aren't Jewish: Darfur, Rwanda, Bosnia, Ukraine to mention just a few modern genocides since the Holocaust."

We were emotionally drained from watching videotaped testimonies from survivors, by the daunting visuals of piles of clothes, spectacles, and hair taken from the murdered to be repurposed in support of the Nazi war effort.

The museum also touched our hearts by its stunning tribute to the slain: six million small stones representing each individual lost to the Nazis' "final solution." It was a solemn visit that both depressed and heightened our senses to the magnitude of the worldwide assault on humanity. At the same time, it instilled our sense of Jewish identity with inspirational sculptures of remembrance of our fallen brethren. A robust flame constantly burned in front of the museum at all times, every day, to symbolize the eternal struggle for life.

Then Ezra continued to pontificate. "What would you do if a society took away your rights to work, get educated, own property, and live? Would you go along like sheep and accept the status quo, or protest in the face of potential assassination? Where were Jews to go, when no country would let them migrate to their lands? I'd rather join the underground than be passively slain."

Then young David contributed, "At the end of the day, we each have one life to make as we want. Do we live for an idea or for ourselves?"

In a demonstrative show of force, Daniel disrupted the numb quietness of the group, "If I were alive back then, I would have kicked some Nazi ass."

"Easy to say," I said. "But what if you have family to take care of. Then what would you do? Abandon your children? What if you were old or sickly? What if you were just a young boy or girl? It's just not that easy to get up and leave or to fight. The six million people who were slaughtered were a gradation of every type of person possible. You have to remember, the Jews were beaten down financially, emotionally, and physically for years…losing their jobs, homes, and were ordered to march for miles and if you stepped out of line you were shot in the head. What would you do under those circumstances? Step out of line and face certain death, or walk along a line that symbolized hope for a turn for the better? The Jews didn't know they were marching to their eventual deaths in extermination camps. To them, going along meant surviving and hope for a relocation and a better life."

Then Aaron offered a new scenario and his own brand of bravado. "The question is if you had an opportunity to point a gun at the temple of Hitler himself, would you pull the trigger?"

Ezra seized on the hypothetical. "That's fairly easy in retrospect, since the truth has been revealed since the war ended and we have had decades of historical reflection. Now it's easy to say, we should have been more organized, should have been more resistant, should have been more willing to fight and sacrifice and maybe millions of lives would have been spared."

"Why don't you join the Israeli Army then? Now?" Daniel challenged as if he had already enlisted and had nothing to prove, then he abruptly left the room.

"Is it necessary to risk our lives for another country?" I questioned, not wanting to simply state that I was not interested in joining any military.

"But Israel is like our home too. It would welcome us unconditionally if we ever needed to migrate," Abigail pleaded.

"But it's stable now," I said. "It's entrenched in its brief but established recent history with a mature military, the strongest and most renowned in the Middle East. What could I add to it?" I resisted. "I could probably be more useful earning a decent living in the US and providing financial help in terms of donations to Israel."

"You mean, throw money at the problem," Ezra summed up.

"Well, they need money. I don't know. Maybe I will join the Israeli Army," Gabriel said. "Daniel said he intends to."

Ezra dismissed that statement. "Daniel is always bragging about wanting to drive a tank and pilot a jet. Yeah, well, it's easy to brag about wanting to join the military; it's another actually doing it."

"So why be a part of the Jewish society if everyone hates us?" Abigail asked. "Why not just conform to Christian culture? That would be a lot easier to join those in power."

"Because being Jewish isn't all about suffering," Ezra explained. "That has been a treacherous pattern in history, yet, despite the many mass persecutions, we as a people have rebounded and prospered wherever we have been forced to live. There's a liveliness to the Jewish culture, one that celebrates all aspects of living. We have contributed throughout history with people like Moses to Albert Einstein. Our culture embraces and celebrates life."

Chapter 4: Jerusalem

After several weeks of sleeping under the stars and hiking through the desert, and visiting various sites throughout the country—Be'er Sheva, Elait, Tel Aviv, Sea of Galilee, Haifa, and other cities—the group stopped in Jerusalem for a 3 month stay. Each of us, except Steven, was assigned to live with an Israeli family as a temporary adoptee.

"The last I heard from Steven was that he complained about his shave. I heard him complaining sheepishly, 'I just had the worst shave of my life.' I knew that seemed an awfully weird complaint about such a small matter," I said. Little did I know, that complaint represented his state of mind. Steven dropped out of the group and boarded a plane back to Canton, Ohio, to reunite with his girlfriend just 3 weeks into a 6-month trip of a lifetime.

I brought my suitcase and shoulder bag and dangling camera up the eight flights of stairs in an apartment building with no elevator. At the top of the stairs an iron gate walled off the apartment with a viciously barking Doberman pinscher on the other side. Uri, a 17-year-old, opened the gate while chiding his canine companion to calm down.

"Hello, I am Uri," he said with a reasonable command of English, to my relief, and a maturity that went beyond his 17 years of age.

"Oh good, you speak English."

"A little, I am not so good with English. We learn from each other. I learn you Hebrew; you learn me English."

Uri showed me around the apartment and led me to his room, which I would share with him. He proudly showed me his music collection and instantly wanted to know what I liked among his stash of CDs. We created a thin bond over our mutual appreciation of the legendary reggae singer Bob Marley. I unpacked and sacked out. When I awoke, I asked to take a shower. Uri said that the shower was over in the next room, but only use the water to get wet, then turn it off to soap up, then turn the water back on to quickly wash away the soap. "Water is a precious resource," he explained in his middling English. Having heard these instructions in the past when we were at the hotel and a brief stay in a kibbutz in the Negev desert, I was accustomed to the practice of strict water conservation.

Uri was hospitable along with his mother, Nachama, and father, Akiva, and little 12-year-old sister, Nirut. But only Uri spoke English in a way that a conversation was remotely possible. He tried his best for me to assimilate. He took me to the park and we played basketball with others. He was impressed by my adept movements and errorless shot making, whereas I would only be considered pretty good by American street ball standards. Basketball wasn't as much an obsession among the young Israelis as soccer was. So, I was able to leverage my many years of playing street ball in a way that elevated my status among these novice players. I stood out as unusual by my deft passes and turnaround jump shots, and rapid-fire dribbling that enabled me to slice through a crowd of defenders and leap up to shoot the ball above their reach.

Uri took me to a couple of parties, where I again stood out for being an American, an exotic peacock, worth admiration before I spoke a word. Some of the Israeli partygoers took interest in me and asked why I had come to Israel. A young, pretty woman who I would never have had the nerve to approach in the US eagerly sat next to me with great curiosity. "How long are you going to stay? Are you going to move here?"

I could come up with little more than "I don't know."

"Life in Israel is very hard, not like the United States," she immediately differentiated.

That comment struck a nerve, however. "Life is hard everywhere, including the United States," I retorted. "The US has more water and land and more opportunity, but the roads are not paved in 24 karat gold. It is possible to make a lot of money in the US, but nobody gives you anything. Most of the society is poor to just getting by, with many homeless visible on the streets of every major city. Mostly those who have money have many avenues to increase their wealth through investments, but for those just starting out, it's very tough to save after you spend for obligations like rent, utilities, car, food, schooling, insurance, kids, etc."

"Okay, you made your point, but in Israel, we don't drive cars much, because gasoline is $7.35 a gallon," she said, making a quick conversion of liters into gallons and shekels into dollars. "So, we just take buses, public transportation, that is cheap here. But we don't care so much about things here. We don't obsess about hair and nails and other silly things like American youths."

"Or, like your health? Everyone smokes here," I said pointedly.

"It doesn't make any difference. We are all going into the military soon. It is mandatory. We are scared that we will be killed early in life, so we enjoy each day now, however we want. If I survive the military then I will stop smoking. Have you seen much of Israel?"

"Yes, my group and I toured for several weeks throughout the Negev desert and northern Israel, Haifa; my group and I saw the Bahai Gardens, and many sites, the Old City, the modern parts."

"Yad Vashem?"

"Of course, we went to Yad Vashem. But I haven't until recently met too many Israelis."

"We are Israelis."

"You don't look Israeli."

"There is no look of an Israeli. We are a melting pot of immigrants from all over the world: Europe,

North Africa, Middle East, Asia, and South America. We are an international nation."

"That's how most of the cities are in the US too."

"So why have you come here?" she cross examined.

"I came with a group of 15 Americans; we are each living with a different Israeli family and going to Ulpan to learn Hebrew."

"Do you know any Hebrew yet?"

"Just enough to ask for a falafel."

She cast a faint smile for the first time. "You will learn. It's an easy language, but not as clear as English, so that's why a lot of Israelis speak English, so they communicate more precisely what they want, and of course for practice. We are serious about things, since we are entering the military. Each of us has lost a father or mother or sibling to war in the past. Living here is a privilege not a game. We are not silly, naïve children. Politics are taken with the utmost concern, because who we elect could result in directly harming our country and our families. We live our lives not to make money, but to survive and be free."

"You seem to imply that everyone who lives in America is obsessed with wealth? We have all kinds in America, from idealogues to those who just want to make money."

"But you can't really be Jewish in a Christian-dominated country."

"Are you kidding? You aren't ultra-orthodox, yet you call yourself Jewish. Most Israelis are secular, yet they are Jewish."

"We are Jewish because we live here; by default, we are Jews."

"You can be Jewish anywhere."

"But here you can live as a Jew in the majority in your homeland free of bigotry."

That struck me oddly. I countered by saying, "While there has been bigotry in the US in the past and some in the present, it is small compared to the population of hundreds of millions of people, half of whom feel marginalized themselves. But I can hardly say I live in fear or suffer from persecution. But in Israel, you are beset by enemies surrounding your nation and have the minority Palestinian issue to deal with. Don't you find it contradictory that you call yourselves a democracy, but don't let the

Palestinians vote?" Not waiting for an answer I said, "I've never had rocks thrown at me or feared my country would be invaded simply because I am Jewish. If anything, living in Israel is a place where you are hated and targeted because you are Jewish."

At this climactic point I believed I had made, Uri called me from across the room and motioned me to come along. I said, "Excuse me, I came with someone who is leaving."

"So what? Anyone here can lead you back to your home."

"Sorry, I actually don't remember his address, and I'm staying at his family's apartment." I got up, said nice meeting you to the gal, and walked through the crowd in a dimly lit room until reaching the front door. Uri then said to me, "Come! Let's go now. The party sucks."

I didn't want to leave. For the first time in my life, I was at a party that welcomed my presence. But apparently Uri was dissatisfied or had some sort of conflict with another at the party. So we split. Since I didn't know my way back to his home, I quickly followed him out the door.

As the weeks passed and we settled into our routines of attending the Ulpan, language school for learning Hebrew, going to lectures, and meeting with the group periodically for updated information about the remaining itinerary, I felt I should make a greater effort to strengthen my bond with Ahava.

I called Ahava and arranged to meet at her adopted family's home also in Jerusalem but too far to walk. She said she was a little lonely too, and that a visit from a friendly face would be great. I took it as a sign that she really wanted to see me in particular.

After hanging up I showered and made sure I smelled alluring by applying my fragranced body lotion, soap, shampoo, and aftershave. Hurrying to get dressed I opened up my box of brand-new, suede shoes; they were soft as a kitten's nose and just the thing I needed to boost my confidence to meet the woman of my dreams. I pocketed my paper map of Jerusalem just in case I got lost. I had never been to her home before, but I knew I had to take a bus. I shut the iron-barred gate behind me as the Doberman barked at my departure as if I had broken in, stole something, and was escaping. I pedaled my feet down the eight flights of stairs that could wind even a healthy teenager. I walked a few streets to the bus stop, which came within ten minutes. When the bus stopped, I eagerly hopped on because I had felt a rain droplet on my head. Sure enough, as soon as I found a seat, the dark clouds burst and sheets of rain came down.

As the bus went from street to street and turn after turn, I tried to follow the movement of the bus to the paper map I had, but the map was a generalized depiction of the city, which omitted a lot of side streets. I was too far behind the driver to see out the windshield, nearly sitting in the very back. I looked out through the bus windows on the right and left, but they were fogged and dripping with beads of rain, impossible to see through. I tried to ask strangers next to me if anyone knew when the main street I was looking for would come up, but no one spoke English well enough, except one European passenger who knew the area. She said it is very far away. So I waited anxiously what seemed like 20 minutes, not knowing whether I overshot the street or was too short. I decided to take a gamble and got off at the next stop. I opened my paper map and the rain did not cease, drenching me and the map. I could only decipher I was too short, so I ran in the right direction for what seemed like fifteen minutes through the pouring rain. I was soaked from head to suede shoes, which were no longer soft as a kitten's nose.

As I was running, I saw a telephone booth. I decided, I had been taking a long time to get to Ahava and she would probably like to be notified of my late arrival estimation. I could also use some better directions to her home. I was breathing heavily from running in the cold rain shower and picked up the receiver and put it to my ear while digging out Ahava's phone number from my wallet. As I clenched the receiver in the crook of my neck, an electric shock zapped my ear and I dropped the phone, jumping back in the rain. Looking down at the dangling receiver, I saw someone had removed the earpiece covering of the phone, which exposed the phone's wires. With the minor shock I received to my ear, and overall discombobulation of the moment, I stood in the rain in a state of confusion. Who would do something like that?

But time was passing, and I was nowhere near Ahava's home. I opened the map once again, but it was soaked and falling apart. I could barely read it. I took off my glasses, which had fogged up no differently than the bus windows, so I could make out the next main road on the map. I continued jogging through the rain for another mile or so until I believed I was on the correct street. I counted several homes and approached the one I believed was Ahava's. I knocked on the door and asked for Ahava. A moment later an old lady came to the entrance and said she was Ahava. I thought: Wrong Ahava, it's the wrong house.

Then I heard my Ahava ask who it was. She saw me standing in the doorway. The skies had just cleared but I was a drenched stray needing to come in. My Ahava explained that I was her friend, so the old Ahava let me in and got me some towels to dry off. After explaining to Ahava what happened, I fretted, "These were brand-new suede shoes."

Ahava replied, "Well, they're still new." We hugged.

* * *

I lived with my Israeli family for 3 months learning little because of the language barrier, only somewhat bridged by Uri, who seemed to know more than he let on. Truth be told, he and I were nothing alike. He was a Don Juan of sorts, engaging in dalliances with his cohort females without regard to consequences. For he too knew he was months before entering the army and life for him would never be the same. His independence and youth would be over, and perhaps his life taken from him by enemy fire. He smoked unfiltered Turkish cigarettes and on occasion hashish, the recreational drug of choice. He floundered, like his peers in high school, with no optimistic outlook for the future. Motivation would only be rekindled if he should survive his stint in the armed services. The resentment was another unspoken barrier for us. Uri would be soon sacrificing his life for the defense of the Jewish homeland. I would be returning to the American dream, university, and a life dedicated to building wealth and experiencing leisure. To Uri, I was a child, spoiled with too many toys, like a car and a terror-free future.

Every week day, I bused to the Ulpan where I reunited with my group as students in Hebrew classes that, unlike my childhood Hebrew classes, were dedicated to teaching us modern, conversational Hebrew, not rote recitation of ancient Hebrew that meant nothing to us. Now we were speaking simple sentences as if we cracked a spy's code. Yes, we only spoke in the present tense, yet the transformation had begun from an unknowing American to assimilation into Israeli society.

Chapter 5: The Kibbutz

After 3 months in Jerusalem, the group gathered on the bus en route to Kibbutz Aleph in northern Israel near the Sea of Galilee. Along the drive there, Sharona provided an overview of kibbutz life in Israel. She held the bus's microphone and said, "About 250 kibbutzim exist in Israel, each ranging in members from 80 to about 2,000. That's about 125,000 people in total nationwide, which accounts for about 2.8 percent of the country's population.

"Kibbutzim are self-sufficient communities of about 1,500 Israelis who live and work under Socialist rule where everyone lives at the same standard of living and contributes to the agricultural and factory work on the kibbutz campus. The kibbutz is run as a business, where the residents work from 5 a.m. to noon or so, growing and harvesting eggplants, mangos, tomatoes, or other produce for export.

"Although kibbutzim were originally based on orchards and livestock, over generations, the kibbutz evolved to blend agricultural business with more commercial manufacturing, such as production of plastics/carbon composites, robotics, and other modern industries.

"The campus contains individual apartments for each of the parents. The children, after their first 6 months, live on the same campus in a communal cabin with an adult caretaker. Parents, of course, see their children whenever they want to. When the children reach age 13, they move to their own cabin shared by only one or two other peers also on campus. At the age of 18, men enlist in the Israeli military for 32 months and women enlist for 2 years. After serving their military detail, typically, they choose to return to the kibbutz to live and work. Everyone has the choice of either preparing their own meals at their apartment or gathering in the community dining hall to eat eggs, chicken, and other staples from a self-serve buffet."

We arrived at Kibbutz Aleph and were oriented by another leader, Amichai, a lean elder man in his early 50s with a frizzy black and gray beard. He welcomed our group and encouraged a productive stay. He then introduced several others and gave a short history of the kibbutz, which was founded before the War of Independence in 1948. Amichai described the virtues of kibbutz life and the challenges for success, and recent evolutions of the kibbutz to more privatization, abandoning the Socialist model. Amichai then said, "Unfortunately, your accommodations have not been arranged fully, so you will have to sleep in the bomb shelter for this week." That raised some eyebrows amongst the group, but after some reflection, where would be a safer place? After the orientation, we disbanded to our assigned "brother" or "sister" among the Israeli teenagers, another immersion into Israeli daily life.

Each member of our group paired with an Israeli of the same age. I was invited to Noga's family's apartment where she greeted me with an open smile and hug, as if I were a blood relation. We exchanged niceties in English. I tried my Hebrew, which was acknowledged as "Oh, you speak a little Hebrew." But then Noga insisted, "Please say it in English," which was a polite way of saying "You are butchering our language. Please stop this assault on my ears."

The conversations proceeded to inquire about family members and how life was for each of us, which was nearly identical given we hadn't experienced much difference as teenagers. Noga, 17, had been working in the pickle factory since becoming eligible to work at 13 years of age. Before entering college, I had been working part-time in pizza restaurants since I was 14. But unlike me, Noga did not earn an individual income. All her efforts contributed to the productivity of the kibbutz, where all profits were evenly divided among the kibbutz residents. Most of the revenues, however, were for upkeep of the kibbutz and its services (food, lodgings, utilities, infirmary, heavy machinery, and infrastructure construction such as roads, the community cafeteria, pool, and basketball courts)— everything to support a self-contained society, with a little discretionary income.

Noga said that she liked her independent living arrangement in a cabin on campus but always found time to visit her parents who also lived on campus.

Noga told me about the entertainment on the weekends, where talented Israelis performed on stage for the rest of the community. Then there was movie night, the swimming pool, and dancing in the bomb shelters.

Noga introduced me to Elena, another teenaged kibbutznik, and suddenly, I was rained upon with more smiles and hugs by this complete stranger, who instantly regarded me as a brother.

The three of us walked throughout the campus so that I could become acquainted with the environment. Mature trees provided a respite of shade on an otherwise hot day as we strolled along solitary roads, rarely used by cars. The tranquility of the campus was accented with hooting owls and other bird songs, and our light conversations.

After a week sleeping in the bomb shelter, we volunteers moved into cabins with a teenage Israeli and another member from our group. I bunked with David and an Israeli named Oded who constantly played with his Chihuahua. The bad news for us was we woke up at the crack of dawn for work. The good news, we finished our day's work by noon and had the rest of the day to fraternize.

The following day, we all walked to the meeting point where we divided up to go to different work areas. Some went to a field; others were on factory duty. Our jobs rotated from week to week.

In the fields, I was instructed to pull out 5-foot weeds, which required gripping the base of the 2-inch-thick root with both my hands and yanking it out of the ground. It took a great, sustained effort to extract just one weed. We continued walking up and down the furrows, stopping every once in a while, to pull out another monstrous weed. My hands became dirty and red with soreness early and just worsened over the hours in the field. "Drink water," we were told throughout the day as the sun rose to its peak, then the work shift was over. I lumbered back to my cabin and flopped on the spring mattress, dirty and exhausted.

After an hour nap, I awoke and cleaned up for lunch. Walking to the cafeteria was not a big deal. When arriving, I saw more of the community. I stepped in line for the buffet and was greeted with hard boiled eggs and toast. A little miffed at the barebones menu of options, I ate three hard boiled eggs to appease my built-up appetite from the physical labor my body was not used to.

I sat at a long-benched table amongst Israeli teenagers and some of my American group and got acquainted. "Hey," I said, "I'm Isaac, and this is

Ezra, Ahava, Abigail, and David." The Israeli's reciprocated, "You are from the United States?" And after a couple of simple exchanges, I knew the other kibbutzniks as YoAsh, Rivfka, Dudu, and Ari.

After we ate, YoAsh, said, "Come with us. We go swimming." YoAsh was a bold young man with a powerful build and charming looks, always with a smile.

"Sure," we all replied, still recovering from our day's work in the fields and looking forward to refreshing ourselves in the water.

At the pool, YoAsh dove in and swam underwater for what seemed like an excessive passage of time. When he broke the surface for air, I yelled out to him, "YoAsh, are you okay?" He smiled and hollered back, "I'm going to do scuba for the Yaltam Operations, next year."

And then it clicked: YoAsh was readying himself for a superhuman challenge in the Israeli Defense Force's underwater force. Only the highest-level achievers become a part of this 100-member unit that is uniquely trained to disable bombs underwater and perform other deep-ocean missions. YoAsh submerged again this time competing with Dudu to see who could remain underwater the longest. They chased each other like two guppies in a fish bowl, until Dudu eventually propelled himself to break the water's surface and immediately inflated his spent, burning lungs with a gaping inhale. Dudu's face was reddened as he lost the physical challenge against the kibbutz's best underwater swimmer, who sustained his stealthy descent below water for another minute or two just to punctuate his dominance in the contest.

Later in the afternoon, the Israeli teens and some of our American group played basketball. The kibbutzniks seemed at ease playing in bare feet, while the Americans all wore expensive name-brand sneakers and showed some coordination on the court that titillated our hosts. Oded referred to me as "Michael Jordan" simply because I could dribble flawlessly and slice through a crowd to lay in a shot, or shoot a perfectly arcing ball from 15 feet out. No matter what we did on the court, in the eyes of the Israelis, we were as exotic as we saw them. We all melded together. The Israeli girls and boys thought their kibbutznik counterparts were too much like brothers and sisters to develop romantic relations with. So when we Americans came onto their campus, we were perceived like unlimited currency. We were flirted with by hugs and kisses and 100-megawatt smiles. Afterall, the teenagers were living out the ends of their youth before mandatory military service. This summer with the Americans was an all-out, nonstop party, giving the illusion we were all living in paradise.

At night the Israeli and American teens sat circled around the bonfire and relaxed as stories were told and Ahava and Brent strummed popular songs that everyone knew. David had his arms wrapped around an Israeli girl. And Gabriel lay on the ground with his head on Hannah's lap. Romances began to bloom that would help define who we were and where our futures were headed.

* * *

On my first day on my work rotation, the factory was muggy, but still better than working under the hot sun. A set of large moving metal parts automatically dropped pickles into cans then topped them with lids. The cans traveled by conveyor belt to be packaged with a label and put into boxes.

Large fans blew on the four of us. The other three were Israelis, and I realized I was completely immersed as one of them. I was instructed to carry an 8-pound can of pickles from the conveyor belt to the worktable, where we round-robbined the cans, passing them to another who brushed glue on a label and slapped it on the outside of the can of pickles. The next person placed the labeled can into a box of six cans. The 48-pound boxes were then lifted and put on a new pallet, which was then forklifted out of the factory for export. This routine went on and on, and on, until we were staring at an 18-foot-high wall of boxed pickles that were ready for shipment to countries all over the world.

A week later, I rotated to the hen house, and spoke to the keeper, Shlomo. "So, this is my first day working with animals, Shlomo," I said to weaken his expectations.

He scoffed under his breath, then said, "These chickens feed the entire kibbutz." But just then as we stood at the front of the penned-in hen house, the chickens squawked in mass hysteria and rushed to the fence at the other side. The mass of chickens was crushing the ones pinned against the fence. Shlomo jumped over the 2-foot fence where the chickens were running as if they were a panicked audience fleeing a theatre engulfed in fire. He took his booted foot and stomped on a shrew until it was a pancake of rodent flesh.

"Why did you kill it, Shlomo?"

He picked up the dead rodent with his gloved fingers and tossed the corpse into some brush out of the hen house, and said, "It would kill my flock. It must be dead. We live because of chickens."

Then I understood despite his broken English. Their livelihood was at stake. Shlomo was a recluse, partially because he had lost one of his hands from a bomb blast while serving the Israel Defense Force. He carried a bitterness with him even as he faced the senior part of his life. With a graying beard and a few scraggily hairs on an otherwise bald scalp, he sat down and poured himself some coffee in a tin cup. "You want?" he offered. I asked what kind of coffee he was drinking. He replied "Turkish. Everything else is baby water." So, I drank a cup of Turkish coffee until the coffee was gone and a mound of what looked like mud remained at the bottom of the cup.

"Strong coffee," I agreed. Shlomo then lit a unfiltered cigarette. He offered me a smoke too, but that I didn't care for, so I just gave my thanks, but no thanks. Then he told me the story of how he lost his hand, not only to impress upon me the dangers of war, but also to segue into the fact that by having only one hand, he needed help with the next chore on his list. He brought me to another barn, which had a 3-foot mountain of manure.

"Shovel this onto the truck." Flies were swarming the pile, and the stench curled my nose not to mention the assault on my stomach. But I followed Shlomo's lead and shoveled the crap to clear the barn.

The next day, I helped carry 20-foot-long irrigation tubes to new agricultural areas. Ahava saw me carrying the pipes over my head along with others. I was shirtless, and couldn't help notice her gaze on my physique. While walking with the pipe overhead, I returned her long gaze, my sight covering her shapely body as if my eyes were massaging her. I couldn't help but come tumescent, which she took stock with a long, fixated look at my crotch. After we finished laying the piping in the tomato fields under the morning burn of the sun, I approached Ahava and we walked dirty and sweaty hand in hand without saying a word.

We returned to our cabins, parted to shower, and cleaned up for lunch. We met each other again and walked hand in hand, this time without the dirt and sweat covering our bodies. After lunch we walked around the lush residential campus, passing little housing units beneath a canopy of shady trees, the tranquility accented by hoots from birds in the distance. We sat at the trunk of one tree and I unpocketed a small newspaper I took from the cafeteria. "What's happening in the news?" she asked.

I read aloud some stories about the space programs, preparation of defenses against northern attacks from Lebanon, elections.

"Are you going to the disco tonight?"

"Where's that going to be?" I asked.

"In one of the bomb shelters."

"Yeah, the teenagers use the bomb shelters as little clubhouses. On the weekends they play music and dance, and drink, of course. They do all the things kids do when unsupervised."

We agreed to see what all the hoopla was about in the evening then parted for the day to rest. On my way to my cabin, I passed the swimming pool and saw David in the pool with his arms around two Israeli girls his age. I thought, he seems to be adapting quite well for a 16-year-old. I had shared a hotel room with him earlier on the trip and had a few discussions. I learned his father was a leader of a strong pro-Jewish lobby on Capitol Hill. And his father had been grooming his son to go into politics. I thought, well, David has the charisma for that, if only he can avoid future scandals with women in the bedroom. I shook my head seeing the headlines thirty years into the future. Despite my wry pessimism, I was actually in awe of David and knew in my soul he would be very successful in whatever he decided to become.

Diana apparently fell in love with her Israeli "brother" she had lived with in Jerusalem and insisted on getting a pass from work to visit him. After so many absences from the required volunteer labor obligations, she was warned multiple times to stick with the program. But she did what Diana wanted and left the kibbutz, apparently to get married to this guy. She was formally kicked out of the kibbutz program.

Gabriel argued with Hannah about him wanting to visit Greece without her. "It's dangerous traveling alone," she argued vehemently.

That didn't faze him as he proudly boasted, "I know 63 different karate kicks, Hannah. I can take care of myself."

"Why do you have to go now? Isn't Israel enough adventure?"

"I won't get another chance to see the coliseums and other sites once I start college and a career. It's just a stone's throw from here. When am I going to get an easier chance to go?" And with that, Gabriel was gone to Greece and then went back to his family's home in Connecticut.

* * *

Later in the afternoon following my nap, I walked across the firepit area to where Ezra was staying. Hearing no response from my knock on the door, I opened it and saw Ahava and Ezra embraced in a hug. "Sorry to interrupt," I said, hiding my heightened alarm and jealousies. "Hey, Ahava, Ezra.

Hey, would you like to take a jog with me around the kibbutz?" I gestured to Ezra.

"Yeah, just give me a minute," and Ahava and Ezra released each other. "So I'll see you at the bomb shelter tonight for some music and drinks?"

"Yeah, maybe I'll bring my guitar."

"I think the kibbutzniks like blasting their CDs of American rock, but do what you will."

Ezra and I jogged around the kibbutz campus down the lonely paved streets that rarely saw a vehicle, beneath shadows of the many trees, across a field to the central cafeteria, and through the neighborhoods of cabins and apartments. Whenever we passed someone, they asked, "Where are you running to?"

"We're jogging for our health," we yelled back to the questioning kibbutznik.

Between relaxed inhales and exhales, we maintained a choppy conversation about what we've liked thus far and who we were interested in. That's when he mentioned Ahava. At the utterance of her name, I swallowed a large volume of air. Then I had to interrupt. "She and I have a connection, I think.

Well, I'm really into her. You know, we've been hanging out together."

"That's news to me. I did not know that," Ezra said, then volunteered, "You know she and I have worked together and had some intimate conversations."

"Me too," I said quickly.

"Look, she and I have gone on dates together."

"Were they just outings, or romantic interludes?"

"You know dinner and movies together."

"So, was there any physical intimacy?"

"Not exactly. What about you?"

"Well, not so much going to places, but we've taken some romantic walks hand in hand."

"We've also held hands and hugged."

"Wow, really X-rated stuff?"

"Then it looks like she's interested in both of us. You just don't hug and walk holding hands with just anyone. Maybe she just hasn't made up her mind for you, you know, exclusively. Maybe she likes the idea of entertaining two men. Who knows what's going on in her mind."

"Ahava and I have a cerebral connection. It's as if she knows what I'm feeling and thinking."

Ezra then drew the line, "I think she and I are going to be a couple."

We stopped jogging. "Look," Ezra said getting excited, but then regained his composure and reasoned, "Obviously, she's in the middle of deciding who she wants to be with. She can't commit herself to both of us at the same time."

"So why should I dismiss my experience with her?" I asked.

Ezra levied his rationale. "I'm not dismissing your perceptions. It looks like she ultimately has to choose between us who she wants."

"But you are going to Brandeis in the fall."

"Right. Going to be a lawyer."

"How does that relate to her? She's a musician."

"My future as a lawyer will enable her to be what she wants to be. Believe me, no woman wants to face impoverished conditions. They want to be taken care of. What about you? You're studying art. How are you going to support her when you won't even be able to support yourself?"

"I'm not set in concrete about being a professional artist. I just like it a lot and can do it, but I like other things too."

"Well, what about religiously. I'm more proficient in Hebrew and come from a family who is very traditional. That's better for raising kids."

"So you already imagine having kids with Ahava, when you haven't even kissed her yet."

"Why, have you?"

"….No. but I intend to."

"Listen you have no future with her. She's not going to put her future in the hands of someone who doesn't have his future figured out."

"But she's agnostic, she won't care how traditional you are."

"It's going to be different when you have kids. You separate what you believe and do with how you want your kids to grow up. Like structure and religious influences. Let the kids figure out how much they should participate in religion once they come of age like we are now."

* * *

After Ahava finished her shift work, she entered the cafeteria and sat at a table drinking an iced tea. She placed a teaspoon of sugar in her cup and closed the lid to the sugar bowl that each table had. Several birds flew in the open windows and perched themselves in the rafters. When they mustered the courage, the birds dove toward the tables and landed near the sugar bowls. One of the birds pecked at the sugar bowl lid until it flipped open. The bird flapped its wings and dunked its head in the bowl for a taste of sweetness, then flew back to the rafters. Upon Ahava's witness of this breach of sanitation, she set her iced tea aside.

I entered the cafeteria, which was sparsely occupied. There were more birds tapping into sugar bowls than people sitting among the vacant tables. But I saw Ahava alone, somewhat pensive, and approached her, really wanting to know where we stood, if anywhere.

"Hi there, Ahava. Soaking up the solitude?"

"Just reflecting."

"On?"

"Just life. I'm supposed to go to Boston University in the fall. But I may stay here."

"Why?"

"It's just so peaceful here. The Israelis like me. They encourage me to move here."

"But what about the army?"

"They say it's not so bad, but to expect to gain 15 pounds." We chuckled.

"But you'll be separated from your family."

"Let's face it, most American teens are emotionally separated from their parents anyway. These kibbutzniks have something going on here, they really have a system, with the children growing up away from the constant assault of their parents."

"But their parents see their children all the time. They all live on the same campus."

"It's different, though. Look at these kids— they're happy and growing up with dozens of others, immediate lifelong friends. Not like in America where you get alienated in high school unless you are part of a pack."

"You weren't popular in high school?"

"No, God no. I had a single friend. It's only since I've been in this group and met the kibbutzniks that life feels full, complete with joy. Bonded within a society that's happy and proud. That's it. Pride. That's why they don't need an easy life. Their pride sustains them, insulates them from the frivolous."

"But they are riddled with problems too. You just aren't seeing it. Take, for example, Elan. His family emigrated from Iran. The other kibbutzniks treat him differently. Prejudice is everywhere and maligns all societies because every population has people who fear those who are different. The Israelis are complex contradictions. They say they have one of the most democratic political systems in the world, yet the Palestinians don't share the same rights as Jews. Now maybe there's some justification for this if you buy in to the concept that Israel is a Jewish homeland. But then why do the Ashkenazi Jews treat the Sephardic Jews differently? Why does the Jewish population fail to empathize with the incoming wave of black Jews from Africa? On one hand, the government saves 125,000 black Jews from famine, war, discrimination, but when they bring them here, they don't encourage them to assimilate."

"America is worse," she said.

"Not for Jews," I replied.

"It just depends where you live." Ahava made her point. "In the red states, there's plenty of prejudice. It's just not in your face type. It's when you turn around and leave that the antisemitic attitude shows."

"Well, I don't live in a red state. I live in a blue state, Maryland. Listen, Ahava, Israel is a hard place to live, inflation is high, you have to join the military, there's the occasional bombing and constant threat of all-out war by enemies that surround this tiny country."

"But I feel alive here. People value each other here."

"So that's it. You don't feel loved by your neighbor in the States."

"Do you?"

"Frankly, I don't want to know my neighbors well. I'd rather value my anonymity."

"Then you don't understand. When we were in Jerusalem, complete strangers would invite me over to their house for Sabbath dinner. That type of connection is not typically practiced in the US."

"I don't know, the army? Are you really going to shoot people, if necessary?"

"I'm certain, once the commanders see me shoot an Uzi machine gun, they will assign me to peeling potatoes."

"So that's going to be fulfilling to you, peeling potatoes?" I asked rhetorically.

"The jobs vary and they are all necessary," Ahava explained. "I just want to be a part of society, not just be a number like you are in the States. When an unknown American is falsely accused of spying in Russia and the Russians imprison them, does the US do anything but say they are negotiating? Years later, the same American businessmen are still locked up. Israel, on the other hand, initiates military action to recapture its citizens, like the raid on Entebbe. After Palestinian terrorists hijacked a jet airliner, the IDF sent 100 commandos to Uganda's Entebbe Airport to rescue 102 mostly Jewish hostages. Not only was this airport 2,500 miles away, but the commandos could expect a military altercation with Ugandan forces. Once there, the commandos stormed the hostage facilities, killed all of the hijackers and 45 Ugandan soldiers. The main thing is that you are not just a number here."

"What about Ezra and me?"

"That's actually what I wanted to talk to you about," she said softly. "Isaac, I can barely see my future two weeks out. I'm all confused right now. I've never felt so alive and connected. Despite all these nuances you raise, I can't see going back home for more than a visit."

"So you would give up Ezra and me?"

"No, of course not. Stay with me."

"I can't. I have a whole family at home. College."

"You could go to Haifa University here in Israel."

"Have you heard my middling Hebrew. I'd never make it through a college by relying on a second language."

"So why not remain on the kibbutz until you have mastered Hebrew?"

"And be what, a farmer? As much as I like the camaraderie among the group and kibbutzniks, and find the whole experience peaceful and fulfilling, I really don't want to be a labeler of pickle cans. I don't want to pull 3-foot weeds out of the farmlands, nor hoist 30-pound bags of onions onto trucks, nor shovel a 3-foot mound of manure onto utility carts. Regardless of the extended family concept of the kibbutz and that everyone is equal in a Socialist society, I want to explore my unrealized potential."

"Which is what, art?" she asked.

"I don't know yet. That's the point. I want to discover it. Maybe by taking a bunch of different college classes, I will find out what I want to do. But I do know it's not farming, which, behind all of the mystique of the Socialist society, that's what you are really doing: farming or factory labor."

In sharp contrast, Ahava quickly pointed out, "But you don't have to pay rent or the myriad of other expenses: car insurance, health insurance, rent, gasoline, food, school, and medical bills. The list just gets bigger and deeper. Capitalism isn't an easy way either."

"It's not for everyone, and it's not perfect, but for those who want to hustle and make more than factory laborer wages, it's an opportunity to see what you can do."

"So, if that's your way forward, life outside the kibbutz provides capitalism."

"But I can't function in Israeli society the same way I can in American society. I work with nuance in English. It's hard not only for native English speakers but also for those who are academically trained in it."

"That comes in time. You would be unique in that way being able to translate English to Hebrew and vice versa."

"What about you? You're a vegetarian who can't stand the thought of killing a cow to consume a sirloin. How are you going to get through an army detail?"

Chapter 6: Ezra or Isaac

Challenged with too many options with too many unanswered questions, Ahava threw up her hands in exasperation. "I'm going to Jerusalem. I can't take this debate anymore."

With equal confusion, I proposed, "That sounded like I'm causing you some consternation. Is it me or the debate that you want a break from?" I hung my head suspecting defeat.

"No. It's not you," she claimed. "It's just all the ponderous thinking about staying or leaving."

"I get it," I consoled. Feeling a rush of optimism, I offered, "So, let's go to Jerusalem together. It will be fun," hoping to still win her over.

From the kibbutz, we stepped into a jeep. A driver, accompanied by a shotgun, took us to Jerusalem for the day. He drove about 90 miles per hour through the occupied West Bank, which was deemed very dangerous with snipers harassing vehicles passing through.

When we arrived in Jerusalem, we jumped out of the jeep onto the sidewalk. "We should stick together. Although it's relatively safe for a single gal, let's go about the day with caution. Agreed?"

Ahava looked at me and feeling my offer for companionship was earnest said, "Sure. What do you want to do?"

"My adoptive Israeli family lived nearby and my 'brother' told me about a little museum near here," I proudly suggested, feeling an intimacy with the nooks and crannies of Jerusalem that only a native would know about.

We walked a few blocks and weaved inward through a subcommunity until reaching a small house with a sign advertising the museum and business office of the rabbi in charge.

We entered and were approached by a tall, thin young man whose suit revealed a name tag with the title of "Tour Guide: Eli." He said he gives a lecture every hour. So in about 15 minutes, he could lead us through the quaint museum and explain the photos and news excerpts to put into context what we would be looking at.

At the top of the hour, Eli gathered a small group of tourists, including Ahava and me, and explained, "These 'news' headlines you see posted on the display canvas show the antisemitic efforts to extinguish the truth about the Holocaust; they are the Holocaust deniers who claim that the Holocaust never happened. They prey on the gullible and ignorant to obfuscate the truth by claiming it all a hoax. Despite the fact that six million Jews and millions of others were killed and their remains found in mass graves throughout Europe. This antisemitic effort occurs despite the Nazis' own copious documentation and video evidence, along with camera footage by various Allied forces of the liberation of extermination camps…despite the living testimony of a generation of survivors, the most horrific systematic extermination program in history is dispelled with the lying denials of those who can't accept the truth. Today the truth is challenged by those who wish to subvert it with alternative news that seems plausible and is believed by the unknowing masses," Eli finished with an embittered twang in his voice.

We finished listening to the young guide and felt crestfallen for this aspect of attack on the credibility of the Jewish history. Eli told us that the owner of the museum was Rabbi Meir Kahan, a former

Knesset representative who held one seat in Parliament and who was notoriously known as a hardliner and Zionist. Ahava and I asked a few questions, which Eli thoughtfully answered. Given our interest in the subject, Eli extended an invitation to his boss's office, which was around the corner attached to the museum. Eli said, "The rabbi takes every opportunity to meet new supporters of his campaign against the Palestinians."

As Eli started to lead them to the rabbi, I whispered to Ahava, "I've heard of him before. Isn't he considered a terrorist even among Israeli political leaders who feel his extremism is damaging Israeli ethics? I think he has organized retaliatory bombings without the approval of the Israeli military." Ahava's eye's widened at my summation, but with curiosity burning through our minds, we waited a few minutes to witness this monstrous cancer within the Jewish state.

Eli waved us into an office where Rabbi Kahan, the terrorist and protector of Jewish history, stood up from his swivel chair and extended his hand. I didn't know what else to do but to reciprocate the courtesy. Not wanting to seem hostile, I shook his hand. To my surprise, it was a warm pleasant handshake that seemed like it was extended from an ordinary person with a heart of gold. I wondered if all men of war and terror carried the same duality of seeming humane, which contradicts their murderous actions. Was Hitler the same? Of course, he was. He was endeared by most of the German citizens. Being able to charm an audience seems like a requisite to exploiting the very same audience. One can't very well rise in the public eye and wield power without a certain amount of charisma. Stunned by my apparent fight between expectations and my immediate sensory experience, I continued to feign interest in this rabbi, who I knew to be outside the fringe of morality. Yet he spoke some truths: that's what contorts his being. He correctly finds fault in being a victim of antisemitism, but his answer is no better. In contrast, the Israeli society has a moral backbone that harnesses restraint whenever possible.

As we made his acquaintance, a stream of bullets shattered the office window, hitting Eli and busting through the cranium of Rabbi Kahan. The blood splattered on the wall behind him as Ahava and I slammed our bodies to the carpet in instinctive reaction to the sudden blasts. Dozens of bullet holes riddled the walls. Eli lay dead with numerous bullets tearing through his suit into his flesh.

Our hearts were pounding. We lay there on the carpet in front of Kahan's oak desk. After a few minutes and hearing the hoots of the gunmen get fainter as they drove away, we rose wearily seeing the aftermath of blood pooling on the carpet next to the rabbi-turned-extremist. His eyes remained open and unable to blink with life. His mouth agape and body with the weight and stillness of any inert object. From this scene of holes through the windows and shards of glass thrust in and around the room, Ahava and I stumbled out of the office in a state of shock, exiting through the museum to reach the outdoors.

The sun was bright and, on any other day, would symbolize a source of life, but at that moment, the bright sunshine seemed too blinding as we gripped each other's arms in an effort to stabilize our stance and senses. A man, regardless of our perception of him, had been slain, assassinated before our eyes. And his assistant too, snuffed out by gunmen who fled the scene. Human beings gone. The questions that should naturally arise such as "Who were the gunmen and why did they resort to such violence," did not occur to either one of us in our confused and shaken state. If any coherent thoughts arose in Ahava or me, they were "How are we still alive?"

Feeling safer behind the museum, we were still inhaling gulps of air as if we had just sprinted a mile until our senses were somewhat restored, I finally asked, "Are you okay, Ahava?"

In a rare outburst of anger, Ahava cursed, "What the Hell; we were just shot at?"

"I don't think we were the target, Ahava. The rabbi is a controversial figure, even among our own. He's led his own brand of terrorism. But there's no way to know who was after them: the PLO, or possibly the Israeli Defense special forces, or may a rogue detractor."

"How can you say that?"

"The rabbi was an extremist that has harmed the reputation, mindset, and morality of the state of Israel. Who knows who took him out."

Police units converged in the front of the office blaring their sirens as canines were let loose to check for explosives and remaining perpetrators. They scoured the office and adjacent museum until reaching the back exit and yard where Ahava and I stood still holding each other in fear. The dogs surrounded us and growled to demand submission. We visibly trembled in trepidation at the canine's vicious barking and show of teeth that could shred clothing and flesh. The police officers recognized the ordinary pedestrian nature of Ahava and me and called off their dogs, who quieted in a withering withdrawal. The officer shouted a command in Hebrew, which neither of us understood but could guess from circumstances that he probably wanted our hands up or to lie facedown. In my rudimentary Hebrew, I declared, "We are Americans from the United States." I could barely conjure any Hebrew any more than the simplest of common phrases in my terrified state. "We speak English," I blurted in English, with my many months of studying Hebrew leaving my brain.

The three cops lowered their guns that were pointed at us and returned them to their holsters, then approached us. We were taken into custody for questioning, which lasted hours, but were released as eyewitnesses to the assassination. We contacted our driver from the police station who picked us up and further vouched for our identities and stay at the kibbutz, should they want to contact us again.

With tiny specs of window glass and blood spatter from the fallen still embedded in our clothes, Ahava and I held hands in the back seat of the jeep all the way on our return to the kibbutz. The fear and firsthand experience of the tragic demise of two human beings seemed to bond Ahava and me in a way that communication or physical intimacy could not do by itself.

Exhausted from the day, Ahava and I hugged each other and went to our separate cabins for rest. We immediately showered in an effort to cleanse ourselves from the horrific shock of the day's events.

The following day at the kibbutz, the only smart thing to do was to address the remaining members of our group of the ordeal and let our driver explain the story to the kibbutzniks. We did this to minimize the number of times we would have to rehash the gory, indelible details.

Sharona gathered the group and, as always, took the lead in saying that an incident occurred involving the assassination of one of Israel's controversial public figures and that it happened beside Ahava and Isaac. "They are here today as witnesses to the happening and survivors of a brutal drive-by shooting. Ahava and Isaac will now address you all to tell you what happened and how they feel about it."

I started with inconsequential words to buffer us from this responsibility. "I don't know what to feel?" Then I managed to address it more bluntly by distilling what had actually happened. "Two human beings were gunned down next to Ahava and me, yet maybe it was for the good of the people. Maybe it's a setback for our people. Who knows whether terror tactics advance one's cause or hold it back. Should we be saddened that our brethren, no matter how extreme, have fallen? Should we feel happy a terrorist is dead? How can I be content with this outcome when I feel so disturbed by our personal association? It's a paradox, like so much of Israel's struggle with its own identity."

After Ahava and I said a few words, Sharona invited the group to discuss the ethics and implications of the incident, which led to a broader discussion about the nature of Israel.

A mishmash of group members talking over one another said in combination and in essence, "How can a country be the moral standard while having to defend itself against aggression from the dispossessed Palestinians? Although Israel gives the Palestinians who have Israeli citizenship the right to vote, Israel excludes all the Palestinians who live in the occupied West Bank, because the Israeli government knows if it includes those in the West Bank, Israel will no longer have a Jewish majority and the land of Israel will no longer be a homeland and haven for Jews. Therefore, Israel must be an occupier of the West Bank and Gaza. And in that role, they lose worldwide sympathy as victims because they are now in a role of dominator and occupier. They lose the narrative that gained international support and established the country legitimately."

Counterarguments followed. "If the surrounding Arab countries refrained from their initial invasion that started Israel's War of Independence, and didn't promote the exodus of the Palestinians for their invasion of the ragtag civilian army of Jews who managed to escape persecution from Europe and Russia, there may have been a history of collaboration and peace. But what has contributed to the Palestinian refugee issue is the unwillingness for the Arab nations to aid them and assimilate them into their societies, causing generational refugees."

Even Brent voiced a stance. "In all this, is the continued fight for the soul of Israel as a place of peace, righteousness, and self-reliance? That cannot be achieved if Israel harbors Jews who engage in the same terroristic tactics as its enemies. For all we know, our own people may have assassinated Kahan like a scalpel removes a cancer."

Then it was Sharona who offered a summation that called to her religious teachings. "We don't know who was behind the murder of Kahan, we are only speculating, and we don't know whether his life was a cancer because only God himself can judge a man's soul."

As the young thinkers hashed out the fine lines of logic, the debate became more and more insoluble. Even Ahava chimed in, "I think you're wrong. While Kahan lived, everyone has a right to assess his value. But no one has a right to end his life."

And in contrast, I felt compelled to offer my take. "But sometimes you have to act in the face of adversity. If only someone could have cut down Hitler, how things may have been different for millions of people."

Ezra then said, "You sound like you are condoning assassinations. That's terrorism."

"Terrorism or freedom fighters," I tried to explain. "It's subjective depending which side you're on."

"No," Sharona interjected forcefully. "The Israeli Defense Force does not target civilians, whereas the PLO intentionally does. We are fighting the good fight for our right to exist; they are terrorists who refuse to negotiate peace, compromise for a legitimate path to statehood. Israel has already shown its willingness to give up valuable land, captured during the wars, for the sake of peace. What have the Palestinians done, but refuse to accept Israel and vow for its destruction?"

* * *

After a few solemn weeks of self-reflection, the two Americans resumed a sense of normalcy working in the fields and factory of the kibbutz. They used their leisure time to interact with the kibbutzniks at the pool or basketball court, and later in the evening, in the bomb shelter to listen to music, dance, and drink alcoholic beverages in an otherwise carefree life.

After 5 months in Israel, the original group of 15 grew smaller once again as several of the members became weary being away from their family and birth home. One by one, members said their goodbyes and boarded an El Al jetliner to return to the States where they could live free of news flashes of bus bombings, suicide bombings in markets, and rocket launches into populated areas. They could take long showers, effortlessly communicate in English with anyone, and enroll in college. They could prepare to earn a well-paying career job and live out the American dream in a large house with a two-car garage.

Steve had been the first to leave. That happened 3 weeks after arriving to Israel. He had left behind a girlfriend who held his mind in a steel grip with the promise of sexual intimacy. Nothing could lure him away from his teenage instincts.

Since the summer was ending, Gabriel left too to visit Greece then returned to the university in America. He said he was in an utter state of confusion and needed to return home to recalibrate his thinking.

After 5 months, Hannah and Abigail, the pretty ones who sang show tunes, left because they had had enough of the heat and physical labor and just missed home. The young ladies seemed to miss home more so, and left at the 5-month mark. They both enrolled in college with majors in Judaic studies. Besides, Hannah pined for Gabriel and wanted to follow him to the same university he had enrolled in.

Diana was kicked out of the program due to her lack of participation in the labor. She got engaged with her Israeli "brother" and took him home with her to Houston, Texas, where her family owned a mansion and her high heels were better served than when hiking through the Negev desert.

Gregory, the autistic fellow, grew his hair long with curly sideburns hanging by his ears, so they appeared like the payos of Hassidic Jews. But despite the effort to copy the most committed of Jews to Judaic ritual, he left at the calling of his family, who worried he was being brainwashed. He actually did not follow any Judaic behaviors. He just liked the image of a respected member of the Jewish community.

Aaron left too, lured back home by an attractive collegiate baseball scholarship. He was certain it was his path to the major leagues. He claimed that if Israel had a professional baseball league, he would make Aliyah. But as there is none, he'll be hitting home runs in the States.

Daniel, who boasted he was joining the Israeli military, went home too. He missed, of all things, parties and getting high, and the guarantee of taking over his father's multimillion-dollar mattress warehouse business. He bragged that he had it made, because within 5 years, he would be running the operation as its president.

David didn't want to leave Israel. He felt perfectly at home and seamlessly meshed with the kibbutzniks, especially his Israeli girlfriend, Dahlia, whom he loved. But despite his family's support for

David to make Aliyah, they equally wanted him to return to the US to resume and finish high school. David's family even said they would join him in making Aliyah, but first he must finish school. With a torn heart, David left after 6 and a half months, vowing to return soon.

Through this weekly attrition of members, the group whittled down to three die-hard members. Only Ahava, Ezra, and I remained. We appeared the most torn and confused. Except for David, who made plans to return to Dahlia, the others got their extended vacation and were introduced to the Jewish homeland and will carry fond memories of the Israelis for the rest of their lives. For us, however, we were perplexed; a calling for duty nagged our consciousness. We were the future nourishment and new blood to contribute to our ancestry and descendants.

That left Ahava and her two competing guy friends: Ezra and me. Both he and I wanted to stop fearing the other's progress for a relationship with Ahava. At this late stage into our adventure and nearing exasperation, I finally asked, "So who do you want to be with, Ahava—Ezra or me?"

But like a politician tightroping a controversial question, she said, "I'm fond of both of you. You each have qualities that I'd be proud to have around me." But then she decided to give an unequivocable reply, "But I have life ambitions and can't be held back by a relationship. You know what I mean. I am thinking of making Aliyah and going to college, maybe joining the Israeli Army. How can I entertain a relationship when so much is going to change for us in such a short time? We won't be able to be together; it would be a distraction."

"Or maybe we can help each other through these imminent turbulent times," I countered.

"That's the thing, I don't want any help. I want to see what I can do on my own. Your generous help would actually be handicapping me…because I would never know what I can do for myself. Don't you see? Both of you would interfere with my future. I want to own my future. I'm just not ready for a relationship with either one of you. Not now. Besides, I could never decide between you two. I have to go now. It's time. I have to return to my family in New Jersey. It's been more than 6 months. I will stay a while and return to my adopted family's house for a temporary refuge and enroll in Haifa University to prepare myself for Judaic studies."

"You are going to make Aliyah?"

"I know I don't like American society so much. It just seems so silly, teenagers thinking about fashion and makeup. I feel important here, and I want to be here and start a family; the teenagers here are old souls, knowing they may have to make the ultimate sacrifice in the prime of their young lives for the sake of survival of the Jewish homeland. That makes every individual an important person, not just a number. Here you can be Jewish and proud. In America you are constantly bombarded with Christmas sales commercials and other Christian influences. I want my life to mean something more than how big my house is or what kind of car I drive."

"I feel what you are saying, Ahava, and if making Aliyah has that much pull on you to part with country, family, and friends in exchange for life here, then so be it. I'm going back to the States," I said, seeing reality clearly for the first time.

Then the truth just came out of me as I expressed myself in a diatribe. "I see Israel as nothing more than a poor version of America, but where everything is hotter and harder. We were lucky to be born in the richest country in the world, where taking a shower is of no consequence to water supplies. You take for granted how fortunate you are not to live in an outright hostile environment surrounded by enemies and internally threatened by terrorism. You don't have to deal with famine like there is in many African countries, or civil war like in Syria, or live next to the threat of a Russian invasion in Ukraine. You have rights that the Chinese don't have and a healthy economy that leads the world. Not that it's a free ride in the US, but at least you can live a life free of horror and limitations."

"But you can't be Jewish in a Christian-dominated country," she pleaded, knowing she was casting a thin argument.

"You can be Jewish anywhere you want," I retorted with exasperation. "Who do you think makes up the Jewish diaspora?" Then the core of me swelled to the surface as I put my essence on the line. "Besides, is it at all necessary to be Jewish? Can't one live a life without organized religion? Do you really need scripture to tell you not to kill your neighbor or can you figure that one out by yourself? Isn't being a good person no different than being a good Jew?"

"I don't know anymore," Ahava admitted.

Then she continued, "Look at these Israelis. They are full of grandiose idealism. And that's not a bad thing. They have established a homeland, converted the desert into blooming lands, and inspired a people from all over the world to come and live in a society that embraces and values them."

Feeling guilty that she raised a good point, I said, "I admit, while their idealism is inspiring and their actions usually realize such idealistic outcomes, look around at the paradoxes. They save hundreds of thousands of black Jews from famine and persecution in Sudan, but don't encourage proper assimilation into their society because of prejudice. Israel is a Jewish state but most Israelis are secular. They say Israel is the most democratic government, but they exclude Palestinians from the West Bank to vote. They say you are subject to persecution for being Jews in other lands, and while that's true in some countries such as Russia, being Jewish in Israel is more dangerous than anywhere else because they are surrounded by aggressive terrorist-led peoples who refuse to recognize Israel's right to exist."

"I only know what I feel," Ahava asserted. "These problems you raise are not insurmountable. In time, they will be resolved. What is known for sure is that Israel is determined to exist for the sake of the Jews throughout the world, whether we come from the famine-stricken Sudan or the wealthy United States. And I intend to join the Israelis' struggle. No one says that it will be easy."

"But I love you." It just spilled out of my mouth effortlessly, without premeditation.

"I know you do. And I love you too. But not the same way you say it to me. I am my own woman. I know you are at the peak of your sexuality as a man; maybe that's clouding your judgment. It certainly weighed on Steven 5 months ago. He didn't enjoy his 3 weeks here, and left."

"Steven was neither a thinker nor idealist. David on the other hand is. David told me he is going back to the States to finish high school then return to Israel to make Aliyah. His family supports him and may also move here too. David's family has a lot of money, which will help their transition here to be more comfortable. I just don't know how he will fair, you know with obligations to join the Israeli Army. He's a vegetarian who would not hurt a mosquito. How is he going to defend himself in a shootout, or against Palestinian youths throwing stones at him? Is he really going to shoot at youths or worse, go to the front lines if war should break out?"

* * *

After all of the arguing and explaining and repositioning, all the members of the group except Ahava had returned to America and their real families to start or resume their university studies. Even David, the most ideological among us, went home.

As university students, we experienced another phase of community living among peers and academic challenges that poked and prodded our perceptions and ideals. We were scattered in Los Angeles, New York, Houston, Boston, Philadelphia, Washington, DC, and other major hubs absorbing new influences to think about. Our efforts for self-discovery may have been titillated by our indelible experience in Israel, but it did not end upon our return to the States.

Over the following year, some of us who lived near each other reunited for social outings. We usually met at David's house, a large, old farmhouse in a very expensive area of McLean, Virginia. Abigail, Hannah, Daniel, and Brent often came to these get-togethers, where we reminisced about Israel and caught up on our latest academic developments.

David was the most antsy, pining to return to Israel. And after his senior year in high school, he took his idealism to action and left his family, friends, and country once again to recapture the magical experience we all found so captivating in Israel. This time, however, David didn't intend to sojourn for a short visit, but rather go to live, serve, and remain in the Jewish homeland for life. We wished him well, knowing he of all persons was ideologically inspired with a passion for politics; yet he was also still a teenager with all the gravitational pull for bonding with females. We wondered which part of him, if not both, was driving his motivations.

Daniel seemed a million miles away from such a commitment. He was more enamored with a 3-foot bong he brought to show off his machismo for getting high. He did that in the backroom with his one other enthusiast, Abigail, while I talked to Brent and Hannah about missing Ahava and wondered if she was doing all right at Haifa University.

For those members who lived too far away for reunions, I simply wrote letters to maintain contact. But who I missed the most was still in Israel.

Ahava and I maintained correspondences over our year separation. And throughout that hiatus, my longing for her grew even stronger, until I was compelled to seek her out with the intention of making my feelings for her known and clear.

I knew I was always welcome at Kibbutz Aleph to work as a volunteer, so as soon as my final exams were taken, I booked a flight back to Israel, this time to hold Ahava in my arms.

From our reciprocal letters, I knew her address. I wanted to surprise her, so I came unannounced. I approached her apartment in Haifa and knocked. Someone answered and told me that I had just missed her by a couple of weeks. She had been here but decided to spend time with a friend at Kibbutz Aleph. She didn't have her number. But knowing I was always welcome there, I took a bus to the kibbutz.

At the gate entrance of Kibbutz Aleph, I explained to the guard that I wanted to visit a friend of a kibbutznik. I knew many of the kibbutzniks from my former trip, so I gave the patrol guard Amichai's name. After getting frisked, I entered the kibbutz's campus and first met Amichai. He welcomed my surprise visit and we sat in the shade drinking tea to catch up on what had transpired with me and the others who made such a bond with the kibbutz. He asked what I was going to do with the rest of my life. And what brings me back to Israel. We discussed that I was in the university studying psychology because that is what had inspired me and that I think I can make a living as a therapist.

I walked to the cabin where Ahava and her friend would be. I knocked lightly on the door but no one answered. The door was ajar, so I pushed it open a bit more and called Ahava's name gently. "Get out," someone yelled from beneath the covers of a bed.

Somewhat embarrassed, I reassured, "I'm not looking, but do you know where Ahava is?"

"She's not here," the voice spoke from beneath the covers in a panicky tone.

I heard more than one voice from the room and was compelled to look again, despite the rudeness of invading someone's privacy. I saw the forms of two bodies under the sheets in one bed. The bedsheet fell from the head of one and there she was, Ahava in bed with Simcha, both now arguing, and Simcha pushing Ahava out of the bed exposing their nudity.

"So this is why you stayed in Israel. You were never interested in Ezra or me. Were you? And your attachment to Israel lay in lust for another?"

"I am just a person, Isaac, not a label. And I have discovered who I am. I don't feel any different toward Israel or you and Ezra, but I'm not that type of woman. I am free to be who I am."

I slammed the door shut and left. I ran through the kibbutz passing the residential units tucked within landscaped trees and shrubbery. I crossed quiet community roads that weaved throughout the campus. I ran past Amichai's cabin and raced by the swimming pool, basketball courts, bomb shelters, and the cafeteria, over a rolling hill until reaching the gated entrance. I signaled to the guard that I was leaving and waited at the bus stop near the kibbutz entrance. A bus came soon, and I jumped on and took a seat and let my thoughts reel. And which path do I take then? Am I driven by carnal pleasures, a material luxury, or ideology? Where will I land in the roulette of life's motivations?

I had thought I must have Ahava; she was the totality of fulfillment in my mind, more than pleasure, materialism, or ideology; or perhaps she meant having them all. Perhaps I idolized her beyond what was real. While her affection for me was genuine, I didn't distinguish between light-hearted romantic feelings and a driving force that would last a lifetime in monogamy. In the middle of Ezra's and my efforts to woo her, maybe she didn't even know her own sexual identity and needs. I don't believe she knew herself what she wanted until now. She wasn't playing with us. She just hadn't fully evolved into her own yet. Just as the rest of us haven't either.

Now I have to cast aside my feelings for Ahava. All that she had meant to me has evaporated, leaving me with just a residual feeling like a stain on a countertop. Our time together just proved I had been there at one point, but no longer, other than a memory.

* * *

I'm writing you, Ahava, now after 3 years since our amazing experience together in Israel. I have many lingering thoughts and feelings about you, but I wanted to apologize. First, for seeking you out without a clear invitation. Second, for judging you. Yes, you are who you are and will be who you want to be. If you are attracted to women or one woman, that's for you to decide. I just can't compete with that. So, I guess I am out of the picture, which is obvious since over the past 3 years, I have not received even a postcard from you. I just find you hard to let go and, in my mind, I held so much promise for us. I now know, from your absence over time, that we are not meant to be together. With that recognition, I am free to move on and free to wish you a happy present and future. I'm glad you are with Simcha, if you still are. She is an interesting young lady. Please let me know what has happened to you since we parted and what your future plans may be.

Sadly, I received a letter from Amichai. It said that David was temporarily living at Kibbutz Aleph as his home base while he served the Israeli Army. Amichai wrote that David was clearing a mine on the road when he and his troops were ambushed by sniper fire. David was pronounced dead at Mt. Sinai Hospital at the age of 19.

I am home now never to return to Israel, for I don't have the Jewish faith instilled in me as a living, burning flame. It has been extinguished with the realities that I care about simpler things. I am not more than a person too. I am just trying to find my lifelong companion, not God, not identity, not community.

The lure of Israel is for people who embrace the history of struggle and the struggle for success as a people in the future. And that is why only the most committed make Aliyah. To become an Israeli, you must be more than tough; you have to believe in something bigger than oneself. And that is why the Jews of Israel, despite the paradoxical complexities, thrive as a union. You must believe that the chaotic dysfunction of individuals can come together as an immovable and unstoppable force of nature to exist, survive, and bloom like a flowering cactus in the Negev.

Take care and be well,

Isaac

Dear Isaac,

For the record, this is a postcard from Jerusalem. Sad about David, but like him, Israel is my home now. I guess I'm a flowering cactus. Take note, if you feel let down by your surroundings, always feel welcome to come here and embrace your Jewish homeland. Take good care of yourself. L'chaim!

Ahava

*A **Postcard from Jerusalem*** features a group of Jewish teenagers who embark on a six-month adventure in Israel. As they explore famous archaeological sites, hike through the desert, and visit all the major cities and attractions the host country has to offer, they all struggle with their emerging Jewish identities and commitment to support their Jewish homeland. While they weigh the pros and cons of making Aliyah, immigration to Israel, they seek to understand their own needs with that of a greater idealism.

About The Author

Cory Schulman has worked as a writer for the past 35 years. During his tenure, he has authored seven books, worked for worldwide federal contractors, and served as a college writing instructor. He earned a B.A. degree from Salisbury State College.

www.ingramcontent.com/pod-product-compliance
Lightning Source LLC
Chambersburg PA
CBHW061123100726
47911CB00013B/657